"Do you know why you are here, Lieutenant Hanley?" It was the first question.

Peter Hanley could answer it. The answer to the question was clear. There was an apartment on Park Avenue, and in the apartment there was a smoky blue sofa, and on the sofa lay a cool lithe green-eyed sort of girl. One of the remarkable things about the girl was her lovely flaxen hair. And another remarkable thing about her was that the hair was wound tightly around her throat.

Her name was Narcissa Maidstone and she was dead.

That was why he was here, in the shaded hallways of the Whitman-Bourne Clinic. The apartment, the girl, the hair, and Death. And him, Peter Hanley. He could have killed her... but did he?

"Ingenious."—*Boston Globe*

Paul Conant Bibliography
(1906-1968)

Dr. Gatskill's Blue Shoes (1952)

As Gene Paul

The Little Killer (1952; reprinted
 as *The Big Make*, 1957)
Naked in the Dark (1953)

"Charged with emotion."—*Newark Star-Ledger*

"Engrossing."—*Los Angeles Examiner*

"Full of suspense."—*Sacramento Union*

"Different."—*New York Mirror*

"Swiftly moving."—*Cleveland Plain Dealer*

Dr. Gatskill's Blue Shoes
By Paul Conant

Black Gat Books • Eureka California

DR. GATSKILL'S BLUE SHOES

Published by Black Gat Books
A division of Stark House Press
1315 H Street
Eureka, CA 95501, USA
griffinskye3@sbcglobal.net
www.starkhousepress.com

DR. GATSKILL'S BLUE SHOES
Published by A. A. Wyn, Inc., New York, and copyright © 1952
by Paul Conant. Reprinted in paperback by Dell Books,
New York, 1953.

All rights reserved under International and Pan-American
Copyright Conventions.

ISBN: 979-8-88601-022-0

Cover design by Jeff Vorzimmer, ¡caliente!design, Austin, Texas
Text design by Mark Shepard, shepgraphics.com
Proofreading by Bill Kelly
Cover art by Carl Bobertz

PUBLISHER'S NOTE:
This is a work of fiction. Names, characters, places and
incidents are either the products of the author's imagination or
used fictionally, and any resemblance to actual persons, living
or dead, events or locales, is entirely coincidental.
Without limiting the rights under copyright reserved above, no
part of this publication may be reproduced, stored, or
introduced into a retrieval system or transmitted in any form
or by any means (electronic, mechanical, photocopying,
recording or otherwise) without the prior written permission of
both the copyright owner and the above publisher of the book.

First Stark House Press/Black Gat Edition: March 2023

1

There was a little wind that blew up from the East River, stirred the stagnant air of the East River Drive, and, crossing the treetops, came into the cool green room where Peter Hanley was speaking in low and rather constrained tones to Dr. Angela Gatskill. She had a habit, no doubt at first professionally cultivated but now second-nature, of gazing unwaveringly into one's eyes, and this made Peter Hanley uncomfortable. But being the kind of man he was, he stared right back.

He also found it unpleasant to talk about himself, especially about such intimate matters as she seemed to expect him to discuss. Sometimes she did not ask her questions directly, but with her deep, searching eyes.

"What," said she during one of the interminable pauses which afflicted their conversations, "has your life been like, Lieutenant Hanley? Just tell me in your own words."

"I always use my own words," Peter said.

"Yes, I understand." Her professional calm was appalling. "Why don't you just start in and tell me what brought you here? Why are you here, Lieutenant Hanley?"

"Why am I here? Why am I here?" He looked at her, then looked away from her, then looked for a way out. It was a hot July day in Manhattan, the sky was a brazen bowl, but here high in this building the little wind of the East River rustled the curtains and kept feverish foreheads a trifle cooler. The room was large, with an air of grace, and the spreads on the maple beds were green like the curtains; the walls were tinted a lighter green, and there were green rugs on the floor.

This particular room was called a "dorm," and in it were three beds. One was occupied by Peter Hanley; one by Dan Brian, the cracked-up Army officer; and one by Milton DeBaer, the rich Jewish shoe manufacturer's son. There were two pictures—water colors of the New England coast—and they were hung with taste beside the windows which diagonally overlooked the East River.

It was hard to believe that those windows were ingeniously contrived so that they would not open wide enough for a human body to get through, that this was a hospital for the mentally disturbed, and that all the doors going out were locked. It was more like the Harvard Club, someone had assured him. Only the white-starched nurses made it seem like a hospital, and even they did not behave quite like nurses.

Dr. Gatskill was gazing at him with her violet eyes. "Go on," she said, "just tell me in your own words ..."

There weren't any words to tell about it.

Could he say that, whereas some men cracked up on dope, others on alcohol, and others on the burning poison of their own hatreds, he had cracked up over a dizzy dame named, of all things, Narcissa? How could he, Peter Hanley, tell Dr. Gatskill about this? He resented her wanting to know. Why did she want to know?

"Just tell me in your own words ..."

"I don't know," he said. "I don't know what got me here. One afternoon I left the Homicide Bureau and the next morning I was here. I remember saying good-by to the inspector, as I do every night, and then I remember you and Dr. Ink-Blot." He shot a glance at her to see if this would get any reaction; he meant Dr. Fredric Holmka, the chief psychiatrist—but Dr. Gatskill showed no change of expression.

"Well," he went on, "I remember you and Dr. Ink-Blot. It was in this room. I had already found out I was in a psychiatric clinic, so by the time you arrived I was ready for anything."

Dr. Gatskill reached into the pocket of her starched white gown and got out a cigarette, lighting it without taking her gaze from him. He ought to ask her, "Why do you do that?" That's what they were always asking him. He couldn't so much as pat his hair or look down at his fingernails without one of these psychiatrists asking, "Why do you do that?"

She drew deeply on her cigarette. "I know what happened to you after you came here," she said. "Why don't you try telling me what happened before?"

How could he? It was all such a mess in his mind.

He sat there. The silence grew oppressive. A fly came into the room and began buzzing around. A tugboat passing the Queensboro Bridge on the northbound tide hooted hysterically. From the tennis court of the college opposite there came the lazy summer cries of the tennis players: "Love-thirty! Love-forty! Point set!"

Peter began to feel the cool clammy sweat on the inside of his palms. What was this damned female doing to him? Why did he feel like this?

"We want to help you get well," Dr. Gatskill said quietly. "Don't you think you could talk?"

"No."

"Are you nervous?"

"Very."

"Would you like something to make you feel more comfortable?"

"A couple of slugs of whisky might help."

She did not smile. "Perhaps we can give you something."

She got up and left with a cool swish of starched gown. She was quite an attractive woman and he wondered why, in a profession requiring such great impersonality, she did not try a little to suppress her feminine graces. But perhaps that was all part of the technique: in the Whitman-Bourne Clinic nobody suppressed anything. That is, within limits.

After a while Miss Dibble came in. She was a new nurse, and professional good nature and severity produced a curious effect; she seemed at cross purposes with herself. Sometimes she was insufferable. She had a little vial and a hypodermic needle.

"What's that?" Peter asked.

Miss Dibble hesitated, and then she said, "Something to make you feel better."

"Dope?"

"Oh, no; not dope, really. Sodium amytal."

"That's dope. Will it knock me out?"

"Oh, no. It will just make you feel comfortable, Lieutenant Hanley."

"I wish it would knock me out."

"Do you?" She administered the injection. "If I were you," she said, "I wouldn't go wandering around the corridors now. Just stay near your bed."

"All right."

Then she swished out with her own kind of starched coolness. There was something about her manner that made him wonder if Miss Dibble secretly hated all her patients.

He sat in the deep green-covered maple chair (just like the Harvard Club) and waited for something to happen. Nothing did. He picked up a book which had been left by some previous patient. It was *Henry Esmond* by William Makepeace Thackeray. He remembered it. He had read it in school. He really felt pretty bright; not many coppers had read *Henry Esmond*. What the hell was it about?

He picked up the book and opened it. He remembered Father Holt, the Jesuit priest, and his sudden appearances and leave-takings at Castlewood. And the young Harry, when first smitten by Beatrix's dangerous beauty.

She was packed with dynamite, too, he thought. There was in his mind another, and more real—was she more real?—lady. Her name was Narcissa. Narcissa Maidstone.

He was staring at the book when three pinwheels appeared before his eyes. They were hurtling toward him, three pinwheels in the darkness. They grew larger and larger ...

Love was, as Anatole France said, *égoisme à deux*: it was a kind of narcissism in which each person found his own most thrilling aspects mirrored in the eyes of another. That's all love was, and when you looked at it, really looked closely at it, you could hardly find it admirable. Brotherly love, Christian love, the love of all mankind, well, that was something else, but the thing that a man and a woman called love—there it was, *égoisme à deux*, a kind of double selfishness.

He was not thinking exactly that, but something like it, when he saw that a pair of violet eyes were gazing intently upon him. It took him a long time to put all the jigsaw bits of his consciousness into a reasonable pattern; and as he sat up, or tried to sit up, he said, "The iron drag of the long days."

He realized that his voice was thick and, when a voice answered, it sounded like the tolling of distant bells.

"Why did you say that?" the voice asked, with its strange, muffled tones. "Why did you say that?"

"I didn't say it. Carl Sandburg said it."

"Said what?"

"The iron drag of the long days ..."

"Do you feel like talking now?"

"The iron drag of the big words," he said. He opened one eye to see if she understood what he had said. He was a cop, but he knew more than most cops. He wanted to be sure she understood that. He had been to school, he was educated, and he didn't want her to think he was just another flatfoot. Well, he wasn't. Not really. And some odd things came back to him now, things out of books, things he had forgotten. Altogether he was in an odd state of mind, for a cop, or for anyone at all. And then when he began talking, he was not sure that he was talking, or whether he was seeing motion pictures on a screen that seemed to jump at him, or whether he was really living a portion of his life again, and time was upside down.

2

"Why are you here?" That was the question that kept coming back. "Why are you here? Do you know why you are here, Lieutenant Hanley?" It was the first question asked anyone here; the answer to this question gave the gauge of the condition of the patient, showed just to what depths went the tangle of the mind. Those who could not answer it at all ...

Well, Peter Hanley could answer it. The answer to the question was clear as the waters of a mountain brook. There was an apartment on Park Avenue, and in the apartment there was a smoky blue sofa, and on the sofa lay a cool lithe green-eyed sort of girl. One of the remarkable things about the girl was her lovely flaxen hair. And another remarkable thing about her was that the hair was wound tightly around her throat.

Her name was Narcissa Maidstone and she was dead.

That was why he was here, in the shaded hallways of the Whitman-Bourne Clinic. The apartment, the girl, the hair, and Death. And him, Peter Hanley.

What was this girl to him? He had loved her and he had hated her and he could have killed her. Indeed he could have killed her. And that was why he was here. The things that went before and the things that came after were all clear enough, but this, the answer to this was not clear at all. He could have killed her, but did he?

Did you, Peter Hanley?

This was the question that had to be answered.

It was the kind of question usually answered in the courtroom, and it was true that the District Attorney would have preferred having it answered there. But there were circumstances, and there was power opposed to the District Attorney—power centered chiefly in the stubborn character of an angular man with deep-sea eyes, Inspector Battle of Homicide. Inspector Battle did not believe that he, Peter Hanley, killed the flaxen-haired girl, Narcissa Maidstone. At least he said he didn't believe it. And yet what was the real belief in that unrevealing mind?

Whatever the inspector really thought, it was clever to have brought him here, a good trick that Battle, almost unaided, had performed. There were circumstances justifying it, some notable circumstances that made it seem the wise thing to do, but the District Attorney did not approve. Nonetheless, Peter Hanley was here.

"Why are you here, Lieutenant Hanley?"

"I am here to see if I can remember—to see if I can untangle the memories in my mind. I am here to see if somewhere there is locked away the secret of how, and why, Narcissa Maidstone was killed. Knowing that secret may set me free."

"Is freedom what you want most, Lieutenant Hanley?"

"Iron bars do not a prison make, but yes. Freedom is what I want most. I want to be free of what hinders me, confines me, holds me back, and makes me heavy with doubt."

The mechanics of it all had been swift, although not too simple, but he remembered it as vague and blurred. He remembered that Inspector Battle, who was his friend, had questioned him at length and in detail. And while the case hit the headlines of the morning papers' early editions and the brass began to clamor for his scalp—the loudest and brassiest of voices having been the District Attorney and Anthony Marriner, the Police Commissioner himself—Inspector Battle had made half a dozen phone calls and here he was. Not under arrest, not charged—although no doubt that would come swiftly enough.

Of course he could have been sent to Bellevue as a psycho—he was certainly in a confused enough state for that. But it was not Inspector Battle's motive merely to have him locked up and out of the way. Rather it was to find the truth. To help him to remember. Battle had had to fight it out with Marriner, the Police Commissioner, and there was a lot of intricate arranging to be done, but at last here he was—temporarily reprieved.

The truth, the whole truth, nothing but the truth. So help me God. Perhaps he, Peter Hanley, police detective, did strangle Narcissa Maidstone with her own lovely flaxen hair. Most likely he did, a nagging logic told him. Else why the blackout, why the reluctant memory that would not yield its hidden truth? What went before and what went after, his mind retained. But the other ...

"And that is why I am here, alone and palely loitering, and no birds sing."

"What did you say?" Dr. Gatskill asked.

"I didn't say it. Keats said it. John Keats."

He wondered if Dr. Gatskill wondered how he knew anything about John Keats. Where did this stuff come from? He didn't know himself; he was in a funny state of mind, and things kept coming back to him, things from other parts of his life. He had got some education crammed into him in school, and some poetry, too, but he had promptly forgotten it. He was a cop; he liked action, not books. How come these things came back to him now?

"We want to help you," she said. "Do you think we can help you? Do you have hope?"

"Yes," he said, "I have hope."

3

He was in a funny state of mind, and the state of mind he was in was called a trauma. That was what he had heard, that was what they had said.

It was dark in the room, the other occupants had gone elsewhere. Probably upstairs, on the eighth floor, in the recreation rooms. That was called "R-T"—for

Recreational Therapy. They were socializing; that was the word, socializing. It was one of the words they had here. Verbalizing was another one.

Peter Hanley, new to the clinic, in a state of trauma and under light sedation, was required to stay in his room, preferably on his bed. Actually, he was glad to lie there, quiet, and without his lamp on. There was only the glow from the light in the hallway, casting a bar of light across the room. Far down the corridor he heard a radio; the music was a jumble of noise in the distance.

He felt confused and alone. He was a man of action, and as he lay there his impulse was to get up, find the authorities of the clinic, and demand to be let out. He wanted to get back to his life, back to the things he knew, the world of fact and action. But the fact was that Narcissa was dead, and the action—the hand— perhaps his, and the idea crossed his mind that he was incapable of going back to his life; he was mentally incapable. The idea appalled him.

But I'm not a psycho! he told himself. *I'm not a psycho.*

He heard footsteps in the hallway, and it was Dr. Gatskill on evening rounds. She looked in at his door for a moment.

"How are you feeling?" she asked. "All right?"

"No," he said, "not all right. Not very good."

"You'll be all right soon," she said. "I'll ask Miss Dibble to give you something."

"I don't want anything," he said.

Dr. Gatskill smiled and went on, and after a while Miss Dibble came in. She had some white pills in a little medicine glass. She moved quietly across the room.

"What are those?" Peter asked.

"Medicine."

"More knockout drops?"

"Oh, no. They'll just make you feel comfortable."

She gave him the pills and a little water after them, then went out. After a while she came back.

"How are you feeling now?"

"Better. A little better." He was, too. A little more relaxed, slightly drowsy, but not really sleepy. He wanted to talk to Miss Dibble.

"Where is everyone?" he asked.

She darted him a quick glance, one that seemed tinged with hostility. What was eating her?

"Do you hate the patients?" he asked. He noticed that his voice was a bit fuzzy. Miss Dibble glared at him.

"What do you mean?"

"Sometimes I think you hate the patients."

"No, I don't hate patients. Not all patients," she said with a short laugh. A trifle forced.

Peter grinned crookedly. He was feeling drunk. "Me? You hate me?"

"No. I don't hate you." She turned to go.

"Well, why don't you stay and talk to me, then?"

"I haven't got time. Professor Bolton is down from the seventh floor and I have to keep an eye on him."

"Professor Bolton?"

She explained curtly. "He was a violent patient. They're letting him visit on this floor while the others are gone."

Peter grinned. "Trying him out, are they? Calculated risk, they call that. I know."

"You'd better stay in bed," Miss Dibble said, and went out again.

Peter fumbled for a cigarette, lighted it, and thought about Miss Dibble. Miss Dibble was a new nurse; she had arrived at the clinic the day after he had, and he would just as soon she had not come at all.

He lay back and shut his eyes. He could hear the radio but otherwise the entire hospital seemed to be in silence. He went half asleep. Then, suddenly, he was aware that someone was in the room. He looked up, expecting to see Milt DeBaer or Dan Brian. But it was neither; it was a very tall man with a long sad face. He spoke in the merest whisper.

"Mind if I come in?" he said.

"Come in," said Peter. "Hanley's the name. Peter Hanley." His voice, he noticed, was even thicker than before. He did not bother to sit up.

"I'm Professor Bolton," the visitor said and let himself down very carefully into the green-trimmed maple chair beside the desk. He seemed tall and gaunt, almost specter-like, in the dusk of the room. After a moment he said, "Mind if I switch on the light?"

"No," Peter said. "I don't mind."

Professor Bolton switched on the light, which cast a slanting beam across his face. Peter saw now that he was no specter, but only a tall and pedantic-appearing man, with rather frightened eyes and lines of tension around his mouth.

"I'm just visiting," said Professor Bolton in a whisper.

"Yes?"

"I belong on Seven. Were you ever on Seven?"

"No."

Professor Bolton let a sharp long breath escape from his lips. "Seven is dreadful," he said.

"How? In what way?"

"Oh, just in every way. Cramped, and cut into little cubbyholes, and they watch you every minute. All the time. I think they even read your thoughts."

"Do you really think so?"

"Oh, yes, I really do."

"It doesn't sound too good," said Peter.

Professor Bolton began a motion of washing his hands. "It's dreadful," he repeated. "Dreadful." He picked up the copy of *Henry Esmond*, turning it over and over, not seeing it. Then he said, "I am a professor of English literature." He stared at Peter and then repeated it. "A professor of English literature."

"Yes?"

"And I am in a madhouse!"

"Oh," said Peter, "I don't think it's as bad as that."

"I am on Seven," said Professor Bolton. "Were you ever on Seven?"

"No."

"Then what do you know about it? I am on Seven, I tell you." Excitement began to rise in Professor Bolton's voice. He kept turning *Henry Esmond* over and over in his hand. He stared at Peter who, though a little thick-headed and somewhat drunk, began to feel on his guard. The policeman's instincts were not operating very strongly in him, but they were operating. Something told him that although Professor Bolton might be harmless, he was getting into a dangerous state of mind.

Professor Bolton's voice fell, suddenly, back to the tense whisper with which he had introduced himself.

"I am a professor of literature," he said. "What are you?"

Peter hesitated a split second. "I'm a cop. A police detective."

Bolton's eyes narrowed, and he whispered, "You're a policeman. That's what the nurse said. I thought she was only trying to infuriate me. All the nurses try to infuriate me. They want to see how much I can stand. Up on Seven they do it, and down here they do it, too."

He put down the book with a swift, tense movement. "I didn't believe her, but you said it yourself. You said you were a policeman, didn't you?"

"Yes." Peter braced himself.

"It was a policeman who interfered with me," he said. "A policeman destroyed everything."

"Yes," said Peter quietly, but on his guard. "I see. How did that happen?"

"A policeman destroyed God's plan," said Professor Bolton, his voice beginning to quiver. "It was I who was to carry it out, but a policeman destroyed it."

"What was the plan?" Peter asked. He kept his voice low.

"Don't you know? Beulah and the children were to go. I was to go afterward. There was the music, the pagan sacrifice, and the drums and the war swords. Beulah and the children were to go and I was to follow. I had the beautiful knife to do it with. It was a policeman who stopped me. Was it you?" The voice had been rising in a fierce crescendo. "Was it you?"

"No."

"I'm certain it was you!" Bolton shrieked. "You destroyed God's plan! God shall destroy you! I am the instrument! I am the knife of the Lord!"

He leaped to his feet and hurled the book. It crashed between Peter's eyes, and he staggered from the blow. Pulling himself half to his feet, he saw Bolton standing over him. The man who was a professor of English literature suddenly looked like a great ape. Then out came the lamp, the cord snapping, plunging the room into darkness. Peter put up his hands to ward off the blow, but the lamp crashed on him. Stunned, he reeled backward, falling flat on his back across the bed. Professor Bolton was on top of him with the savagery of a wildcat. Peter could hear the frenzied breathing, and then he felt fingers at his throat.

"I am the knife of the Lord!"

Peter was far from clear-headed, but his body answered subconscious commands and his training instinctively asserted itself. His knee jabbed into the man's groin. He heard a cry of pain and the long fingers relaxed. Peter followed his advantage and swung with his fist. The blow connected and the professor tumbled back over the maple chair with a crash. Then he was still.

Peter, switching on the ceiling light, heard running footsteps in the hall. Dr. Gatskill came in, followed closely by Miss Dibble.

They both stood still for a moment taking in the scene. Dr. Gatskill's breathing was rapid, but her voice was calm. "Are you all right?"

"Oh, I'm all right," Peter said with a silly grin. He still felt a little drunk.

"You'd better get back into bed then."

Two orderlies came in and, at a nod from Dr. Gatskill, picked up the inert form.

"How did you happen to leave Professor Bolton alone on the floor?" Dr. Gatskill asked Miss Dibble.

"He seemed to be all right. I had to go up to the recreation room with a message for Dr. Hunter."

"You should not have left the floor under any circumstances. You knew his case history, you knew he must be watched at all times. Didn't you?"

"I'm sorry, Dr. Gatskill." And she really sounded sorry.

"It's too late to be sorry. Now would you please go back to the office and wait for me?"

4

He slept, but while he slept he had the impression Dr. Gatskill was at his bedside. He dreamed, and it seemed to him that while he dreamed he was trying to tell Dr. Gatskill what his dreams were about.

The place was the Californian Room of the Alhambra, and he could not say exactly how he got there. It was an odd place for a cop to be, even the kind of cop that he was. So what was a cop doing in the Alhambra, which cost too much money, and here was this babe opposite him, with straight flaxen hair and a look that said most anything you wanted it to say.

"Narcissa," he said. "Narcissa."

"You say it very prettily," she said.

"I love saying it. I love saying it over and over again."

"Do you?" A little cascade of happiness came tumbling into the green pool of her eyes.

"Narcissa," he said.

"What?"

"Nothing what. I'm just saying your name over and over again."

"That's nice. Shall we have another daiquiri? I love daiquiris."

"Yes. Daiquiri us another, Narcissa. Oh, Henry, or whatever your name is, Narcissa calleth thee."

"Don't be antique," she said. "Or whatever it is you're being."

"I'm not antique. I'm modern. I'm antic but not antique. Get it?"

"No."

Henry brought the daiquiris. The frosting was cool,

the glass was cool, a daiquiri was a cool proposition. So was Narcissa.

"Narcissa," he said. "I think I love you."

"That is not a statement which would sweep many girls off their feet," she said.

"I didn't intend to sweep you off your feet. When I said I think, I meant I think. I don't know. Frankly, I don't know what love is. Do you?"

"You're out of your mind," she said.

"Have you just noticed?"

"No. Let's get out of here."

"All right, Narcissa. Come on. Let us go where twineth the woodbine."

Outside the air was sharp and clear, and Park Avenue had an etched look, and it almost made you think of Paris, but not quite. No place really made you think of Paris but Paris. They did not find where the woodbine twineth.

The words came sluggishly. He emphasized them. Then he looked up and recognized Dr. Gatskill.

"We did not find where twineth the woodbine," he said. "Do you understand that?"

"I understand that." The voice came softly, like distant bells.

He was a little boy and out of nowhere came the large figure of a woman, and her voice boomed at him. "Peter!" she cried. "Why did you do it?"

He ran away and hid in a cluster of hollyhocks that grew like weeds beside the corner of the tenement where he lived, and she came and dragged him out. "Why did you do it?"

"I didn't do nothing," he said. "I didn't do nothing. Mom."

"A taste of the razor strop will just about fix you,"

she said.

"I didn't do nothing, Mom."

Then she took him to where the razor strop hung behind the kitchen door.

"And then what?" Violet eyes asked the question.

"I don't know what. There isn't any more. The iron drag of the long days hath me in thrall."

In thrall. Sodium amytal. Not a bad rhyme. John Keats could have used sodium amytal. Purple, it was purple, sodium amytal was purple, and it stained all your mind with a purple stain....

He went up the stairs to that fancy apartment where Narcissa lived. She was only one flight up and it was always easier to use the side stairs than to wait for the elevator in this Ritzy apartment house to be free. Swank, the newspapers would have called it. Or plush. In England they said posh. A swank girl in a swank apartment. Narcissa, from Montreal. What was there in her, a strain of the old French, a dash of Versailles or Montmartre, or was it a bit of Pigalle?

She was wearing what was, he supposed, called a negligee, and she grinned at him.

"Hello, copper," she said.

"Hello yourself."

"You want a drink? Or a cup of coffee?"

"I don't want anything. Drink to me only with thine eyes."

"I can do that."

He kissed her. How wonderful he felt, but only for a moment, for then he remembered why he had come. He backed away from her and sat down on the sofa, which reflected her good taste and also reflected quite a lot of money. Too much money for a poor working girl.

He wanted to say something bitter but all he could think of was: "You're an expensive dish for me, baby."

"I'm an expensive dish for anyone," she said. Her eyes narrowed, and the green flashed in them, but it was not strictly what you call a green light; psychologically speaking, it was a red light. There was a red light in his own mind, too. And then, as he stood facing her, and the traffic roared outside, he told her what was bothering him. He was not quite sure what it was, really, that was bothering him, but he had a pretty good idea.

"I thought you and I were going to get married," he said.

"I thought so, too," she said, "although, come to think of it, that was something for the future. Anything happen to change your mind?"

"No. I haven't changed mine. Have you?"

"Why, no, honey," she said, and she put her hand on his forehead as though testing for fever. "I think you're not feeling too well," she said. "Would a double Scotch help?"

"No," he said. "A little love, a little kiss."

"Guys go off their rockers in funny ways," she said.

Then he said, "I'm a copper. You knew that, didn't you?"

"Sure I knew it."

"Coppers are trained to add two and two and usually they get four. But when they get four and a half, or five, they can generally add that in somewhere, too. Do you follow me?"

"No-o-o. No, I don't."

"I am adding up four and six and I get thirteen and a half."

"I see," she said gravely.

"Who was that gentleman I seen you with last night?

That was no gentleman, that was my sweetheart. Paramour, inamorata. I used to know a Hearst writer who loved the word inamorata. He got it into every story he wrote except the tax rate."

"What are you talking about?" Her eyes were sullen.

"You know well enough. There's something not exactly on the level about you and I don't know what it is. And I want to find out."

"Not on the level?"

"That's what I said. To be frank, there's somebody else."

"It's in your imagination," she said.

"No, not my imagination. There's some character hanging around you and you're taking great pains to hide it from me."

"What makes you think so?"

"I don't think so. I know so."

"Oh?"

"I hate slyness. I hate being deceived. If you want somebody with a barrel of money, all right. Go take him. The hell with it."

"Oh," she said. Her chin went up a little as though he had hit her right on the point of it.

"I don't know who he is," Peter said, "but if you want him, take him. Don't try the double-cross. Not on me."

The little pointed chin was up and the eyes were green as bottle glass. They said nothing.

Then he left. He remembered shutting the door so hard that a pane of glass shattered and when he got to the bottom of the stairway the little splinters of glass were there ahead of him.

5

Inspector Battle looked about as you'd expect a guy with a name like that to look. He was a New Englander, and there always walked beside him the shade of an ancestor who was a parson to the whaling men of Nantucket.

"You're not yourself these days," he said.

"I know it," Peter replied. "I'm somebody else. Two other people. As a matter of fact I'm seven guys in an eight-man squad."

"You're what?"

"The corporal is missing," said Peter. "AWOL."

"Oh."

"Do you want me to do something here?"

"No. I think you had better go home and get some rest. You need rest pretty badly."

"All right."

Then he said good-by and went out the door marked *Homicide Bureau* and there was a little old man sitting on a bench there and Peter thought the man gave him a very peculiar look, but he did not remember it very long because, in fact, he did not remember much of anything after that. Just the peculiar little old guy sitting on the bench giving him a peculiar look.

He also thought he saw Anthony Marriner talking to George Scott in the corridor. Why either Scott or Marriner would be in the Homicide Bureau he did not know, but after he passed the little man with the peculiar look he was sure he saw Marriner and Scott talking to each other, quite earnestly, at the corner of the main corridor.

Anthony Marriner, the Commissioner of Police; and

George Scott, his secretary.

Anthony Marriner was a big bluff man who had made his money in investment trusts and who had, happily, put some of it on the right horse; that is to say, the incumbent mayor. The police commissionership was his reward.

And George Scott, his secretary. Executive Secretary, the title was, but with his insignificant appearance and manner he was more like a clerk.

What were they doing here, in the corridor of the Homicide Bureau?

The little old guy on the bench had given him a peculiar look, and as he passed Marriner and Scott, Scott gave him a quick glance. Friendly—and yet searching.

He remembered the little old guy and Marriner and Scott—or thought he did—and he remembered Narcissa dead on the sofa with her flaxen hair wound around her throat. He remembered going into the street and getting the uniformed policeman, he remembered that his pistol was taken away from him. He remembered talking to Inspector Battle. And that was about all.

The next thing he could remember he was in this room. It was morning, apparently, but this seemed to be the south side, and it was darkish and cool. It was May or June. Perhaps June.

He was sitting on the corner of his bed; his own bed, he guessed, and he was in his pajamas but the other two men in the room were dressed.

"Good morning," one of the men said briskly. "I'm Dan Brian. This is Milton DeBaer. You saw us last night but I guess you don't remember. You were out colder than a potato."

"Was I? How did I get here?"

"Oh, I don't know," Brian said. "I know how I got here and that's about all. By beating up my wife, that's how. She's a little North German whore anyhow, and she had it coming to her, so I don't see anything nuts about that. But then there was quite a hassle and they got my father into it and he was just waiting for the chance to slap me in somewhere. He's an Army officer and he raised me to be one and I guess he's disappointed I didn't turn out to be a major general. Best I could do was first lieutenant. If there's anyone could unbalance me it's my father. Now I suppose you want to know how Milt got here ..."

"Well—yes, I suppose so."

Milt DeBaer looked sheepish and then turned away. You could see he wasn't happy being an inmate of the place, even though he was on Four, which everyone said was a very nice floor—just like the Harvard Club. DeBaer, young, full-chested, with jet black hair combed straight back, contrasted oddly with Brian, who was slender, almost fragile, and who had a sandy complexion.

"I got onto the wine," Milt said, cracking his fingers. "That was what did it. I was all right when I was drinking a quart of whisky every day. But when I started the wine I kind of went to hell in a handbasket."

"I see," Peter said.

"He ain't really nuts," Brian said scornfully, "he's just an alcoholic. That ain't really nuts. Now me, I could be a schizophrenic, I guess. My doctor says all my thinking is ambivalent. I didn't come here for the garden party. I'm really cracked."

Suddenly Brian lay down on his bed and began sobbing. But a few moments later, when a chime rang to announce breakfast, he was up off the bed and away down the corridor like a shot.

Peter Hanley followed, and with him went Milt DeBaer, who kept wringing his hands and saying, "If I'd only stuck to that quart of whisky …"

He remembered all that.

"What happened after you said good night to the inspector?" asked Dr. Gatskill. The question sounded familiar; he thought he'd heard that question before.

But what the hell, he couldn't remember.

"I'm just a cop," he said, and he heard his own words coming back, thick as a piece of French bread, from the other side of the room. He sat up on the edge of the bed and cursed the sodium amytal. "Damn stuff makes me drunk," he said. "Can't you get me some black coffee? Don't like being drunk."

"You don't feel too badly, do you?" she asked. "Now I want you to try to remember more. Talk. Don't try to remember, just keep on talking. How did it all begin?"

It was a day in May. The May before this last May. He was on the Hassenpepper case and that was one of the dizziest he had come across. Julius Hassenpepper had been murdered in the Breakstone Apartments on Park Avenue just opposite the Armory. When he finished with that case and had seen Shorty Cerwin sent on his dreary road to the electric chair, he went back to look at some final details, and there she was, the girl with the jade-green eyes. She was on the stairway and he was too—it was the same, the very same stairway where on a later day the pane of glass fell tinkling down before him.

It was the smile she had, one to write home about, one to write a song about, and any copper who would not be smitten by that smile would not be a member of the human race. She turned it on him full blast.

"You're a police officer, aren't you?"

"Yes," he said. "Why do you ask?"

"Because I'm in a little trouble myself—and I need help. I need to talk to someone like you."

"Well," he said, "I'm someone like me."

"You're very whimsical," she observed. "Won't you come into my apartment?"

Why, yes, he would. And he did. It had the smoky blue sofa which he was to know very well. He sat down on the sofa.

"Do you read poetry?" she asked.

Oh-oh. There's the pitch. When a babe asks you if you read poetry you want to hang onto your hat. The worst is yet to come. She sat down on a chair opposite him and crossed her legs. He did not read poetry to speak of.

Her problem was something quite minor. Just now he failed to remember what it was. But whatever it was he helped her to solve it. And very soon thereafter she became his problem.

There was a word for it. Peter Hanley was in love.

Then the violet eyes came back and after a while Dr. Gatskill said, "What was the problem?"

"I don't know. I can't remember." Remember, remember. Not only the not remembering bothered him; if his hands were clean, why should his mind bury the remembrance?

Dr. Gatskill said, "Perhaps you will remember better the next time."

The eyes grew very small and then disappeared. Now there were only the cool distances of the room and he could feel the fluttering little wind off the East River.

I'm no longer angry, he said. I don't hate her anymore. Where the poison brimmed over in my brain now there is only a stillness, an emptiness. There is nothing left.

And what is ahead? No man may live without hope, and no man may live without love, and both hope and love are gone.... O dead loves of all the ages, where now is thy fire, where now the hot passion that joined thigh and thigh, where now the gasping breath? Where is Hipparchia, where Helen, where Isolde, where are they now and where are the snows of yesteryear? The sodium amytal hath a purplish poison in the brain; it pervades all, and all it pervades it sickens. And if this be truth, let us have no more truth. The truth is a bitter fruit which groweth on a bitter tree.

Three pinwheels came toward him in the darkness, and when he awoke it was gray and there was the beginning of dawn beyond the East River.

What was the future? The question still pressed on his mind. The hell with the future, what of the past? he asked himself.

There was a whole night that he could not recall—or, and the horrible suspicion welled up in his mind like the poison of a polluted spring—was it one night, one week, one month ... or a year?

Once he knew a newspaperman—a police reporter on the *Daily Mail*—who was in the yearly habit of going on month-long binges. But when he was over them he always showed up in the press room, shaking his head and saying, "That was a terrible day I had yesterday."

Had something like this happened to him?

There was an answer somewhere. But he was afraid to look for it. He dreaded it.

6

At ten o'clock that morning Dr. Gatskill came back. She looked just as she had the day before. But now she had a writing pad and a pen. Brian and DeBaer had gone to the garden with the others, and Dr. Gatskill closed both doors to the "dorm." She sat down, crossed her legs, and waited.

"How do you feel?" she asked.

"Terrible," he said, "terrible. I've got a hangover. Sodium amytal hangover."

"It will wear off." She shifted her pen. "Now today," she said, "I want you just to talk to me. Tell me what's on your mind right now."

What he was thinking about was the curious incident of Professor Bolton, and he was thinking that perhaps Bolton's homicidal attack on him was deliberate, was somehow a planned attempt to kill him. Could it be that, in the seeming safety of this clinical sanctuary, he was in constant danger, and worse, in danger from forces that he did not understand? His detective's brain nibbled at something. If the attack were premeditated, if someone wanted him out of the way—why? Because he knew something? So he shouldn't remember?

The violet eyes were gazing steadily at him. Remember! Remember! "In my own words ..."

The morning was a New York June morning. The sound of the traffic was no longer a roar but a lazy hum. Somewhere there was the memory of the bees, and the countryside.

What was there to remember?

There was a time somewhere else—years before

Narcissa—when he was a kid on the East Side. He grew up hating cops—all cops—until he met Sergeant Quinlan, and Sergeant Quinlan "took the lad in hand," so to speak. Then he thought he too would become a cop, and that is what he became.

A cop! A pretty good cop.

So what happened?

He went rapidly up the ladder—too rapidly, some said, and as a lieutenant on the Homicide Squad he began getting his name in the papers. He appeared in every first-class murder investigation and he was quoted on this and that. It didn't go to his head exactly—well, yes, he had begun to get a very good opinion of himself. He could see that now, and it was possible he began to believe what they wrote about him. *Hero Cop* they called him once in a while—*Hero Cop* when he shot that rat in Grand Central and *Hero Cop* when he fished the kids out of the river in December, and nearly went down himself. *Hero Cop* ...

That was part of the buildup—there was a buildup, he could see—and when he began to feel he was cutting a figure in the town he thought he needed to put up more front. He got to know a lot of people who were loaded with dough, and what kind of dough it was could hardly be termed any of his business. Sometimes he did them little favors, nothing much, just trifles, and if they wanted to give him presents, who was he to turn them down?

He bought a new house for his mother. It was quite a sight to see the look in the old lady's eyes when she saw it, but the next look was not so good.

"That's a lot of money," she said. "Are they paying policemen that kind of money these days?"

She was a fattish old lady with the keenest eyes he had ever come across. He could not return that gaze and he didn't try.

"No," he said. "They're not paying any more than they ever did."

"I didn't think so," she said.

"Well, I've got a pal in Wall Street," he said, "and he gives me a tip here and there."

"I never thought," his ma said, "that pals in Wall Street were for coppers. Wall Street and the ponies are not for coppers. Them two things I know …"

"Maybe you're right," he said.

"I'm always right."

But his mother liked the house and later he bought her a car and she liked that, too. Well, the money wasn't really dishonest. There was plenty of dishonest cash around, but he wanted no part of that. The money he took was only for little sidelines. There was the Humber divorce case, for instance. It was a private detective's job, but there was no reason why he shouldn't do it on his own time, was there? It paid him a lot of money, and in the long run it did everyone a good turn. It was about time somebody caught up with Fay Humber.

After that, he was quite in demand on similar cases. And there were other little things, too. Jewelry robberies, for instance, which were getting the routine treatment by the Department. No reason why he shouldn't work on these on his own, was there?

Well, not much of a reason. And how could anyone live on a policeman's pay in the manner in which Peter Hanley wished to be accustomed?

In a way he was satisfied with the way things were going, but not altogether. There was something besides money—another crown which he desired deeply.

What was it? Love? Whatever that was....

"Do you think"—she lay in his arms and looked up at him with green eyes—"that you got the right man in the Hassenpepper murder?"

Her tones were dripping with coolness and disinterest. He was in love with her but he was still on Homicide, and the way people said things—even when they were said lightly, with disinterest—sometimes meant as much as the words themselves.

"What do you mean, the right man? We sent Shorty Cerwin to the chair, didn't we?"

"It wouldn't be the first time an innocent man went to the chair," she said lazily.

"What does that mean?"

"Nothing," she said. "Nothing."

His mind shot back to the first day he had met her, when he had gone back to the Hassenpepper apartment. Was it an accident that she had met him on the stairs?

He looked at her intently, into the fathomless green of her eyes.

"What do you know about the Hassenpepper murder?"

"Nothing," she replied. "Absolutely nothing. If I did, would I be asking you questions?"

The incident was forgotten, at least it was put in the back of his mind.

Everything was put in the back of his mind except for one thing: Lieutenant Peter Hanley was in love. Everything went under that emotion, behind it, overwhelmed by it, smothered by it. He worshiped at the altar of a goddess who had swept into his life like a ship in full sail, had carried him away, and yet—he did not really know her. What was he following, really following, Narcissa, or God, or the Devil? What was it that really enslaved him, her cool and guarded beauty, or the Eldorado that exists in the heart of every man?

He did not know.

June turned into July, and August into September. The autumn rain came down on the home-rushing crowds at Broadway and Trinity Place, on the kids playing dirty-faced in the street at 78th Street and Second Avenue. Time stood still, or moved, and space was bent along with time and light.

He asked her to marry him. He, Peter, asked her, Narcissa.

This happened in Central Park, and it was September, golden September complete with squirrels and sparrows and lazy airs of fall and fall's slowly reddening colors. It was not a place where they often went. She was not a park kind of a girl, and he was not a park kind of guy, either, for the matter of that. But there they were.

"Why don't you marry me?" he asked. He was not looking at her, as might have been expected of a man asking such a question. But then she laid a cool slim hand on his and he did look at her. Her look was almost tender, and in her this was a bit surprising.

"Marriage," she said, "is quite a big thing."

"Too big for us?"

"Yes."

"You don't know what you're talking about," he said. She looked at him intently, with a look in her green eyes that was for once not glittering but almost human. "Better than you do, Peter."

"How?"

"You're in a fog. You don't really see me. You don't know me. You've made some kind of a crazy dream around me, and that's a little odd, too, because you're a cop and in most things you're pretty hardheaded."

"Hardheaded and softhearted," he said with a grin.

"Now be serious. God knows I don't like being serious any more than you do, but you're making me be serious."

She let go his hand and stared across the park. She did not speak for a moment and when she did, her tone was deeper, with some warmth in it.

"You don't really know me, Peter," she said. "If you did, you wouldn't like me."

"Don't give me that nonsense."

"It isn't nonsense. There are too many things about my life you wouldn't like, Peter."

"Such as what?"

She did not reply for a long time. And then she said, "For one thing I know too many people on the wrong side of the street. The wrong side of the street for a cop, that is."

"I know quite a lot of people on the wrong side of the street myself."

"That's different."

She sat silent, cool and more unapproachable than ever, and then she said, "You're a hell of a nice guy, copper."

"That's what the gal says when she turns you down. What the doting wife says when she begins to dote on somebody else. You're a hell of a nice guy. You're a hell of a nice guy, but— And that includes me out."

"No, it doesn't. Not at all. But before we talk of getting married, let's think about it a long time, and let's get to know each other."

"We know each other as well as anyone does."

"We really don't, Peter."

"But—"

"Let's talk about something else," she said.

"Let's talk about you and me."

"Let's not."

She got up, took his hand, and looked into his eyes. He wondered how she could have such a tender look when she had said what she had said.

They walked south in the park toward Fifty-ninth Street.

7

Time got out of hand, went here and there, ran around in circles; and whatever this thing was in Peter Hanley's heart went around in circles, too. It raced madly but got nowhere. Like the wind, it came and went and September became October and October became November and the wind blew cold in Manhattan's crevices.

The thing pursued him; it was a great cat with eyes like jade and it lay in wait for him at night and clawed him with claws of steel. Peter Hanley no longer knew what he was doing. Only he could not shake the name of Narcissa that clung to him.

She was burning around his head like St. Elmo's fire, and yet she was not there—a will-o'-the-wisp, a salamander. He held her in his arms and yet he did not hold her; the lithe body like a willow wand yielded to him, but she was not there, she did not inhabit this body, and it was her absence and not her presence that always lured him on.

There came an end to this. And the end was somehow inextricably tangled with the evening when Inspector Battle said good night to him and he walked out of the door marked *Homicide Bureau.*

Dr. Gatskill's eyes were deep and questioning. "Just talk," she said. "Don't try to remember."

Peter Hanley lay on the green coverlet of the bed,

and the empty ampule marked *Sodium Amytal* lay on the table beside him.

"I said good-by to Inspector Battle."

"Yes?"

He paused a long minute.

"Speak to me of how you miss me," he said. "Tell me of the iron drag of the long days."

The watchful eyes receded and then came back. There was a droning sound in the room.

"It's hot," he said. "Very hot, Doctor. Am I burning in hell? Would I be burning in hell, Doctor?" It was an important question and he hoped she would tell him the truth.

"No." Then she said, with a peculiar intensity, the sound of her voice driving through the lazy summer buzzing in the room, "Do you think you ought to be burning in hell, Mr. Hanley?"

It waited a long time behind the high barriers of his mind, and then it came with such an explosion he thought the green walls would fall down around him.

"Yes!"

The walls did not fall. No fires broke out in the curtains or within the tinsel avenues of his brain. He lay back and said, "I am very hot and burning in hell."

The buzzing sound grew loud, dimmed, faded. The violet eyes, the bell-like voice, and a pair of blue shoes. Why was Dr. Gatskill wearing blue shoes? Everything else was white, except for the violet eyes; the gown was white and the skirt was white, but Dr. Gatskill was wearing a pair of blue shoes. Why? How could Dr. Gatskill's blue shoes have any meaning to him? For a moment they seemed to have. Then three pinwheels began dancing in the darkness; they whirled and spun in the darkness....

Once upon a time there was a Georgian house. It

had green doors and white shutters. But the shutters were only the fancies of an architect; they did not shut. Neither did they open.

"Nothing opens," he said.

"Don't try. Don't try to think or remember. Just talk."

The pinwheels danced off in the darkness and the green Georgian shutters, which were only an architect's fancy anyhow and not designed to open, began to unfold like the wings of a butterfly.

"Some men do it with a kiss, some with a sword ..."

The probing eyes were very bright. "What did you say?"

"I didn't say it," he said. "Oscar Wilde said it."

"I know who said it. Some with a kiss, the brave man with a sword." The eyes came very close. "And you?"

There was a motion picture screen before his eyes. The words came up slowly and the words burned in terrible letters of fire. "YOU? YOU? YOU?" The words filled the whole room.

"There was a blackness in my soul," Peter said. "Do you understand that? A blackness in my soul—and it was named hate."

"Yes, I understand."

"She was not there anyway. There was no Narcissa in that body. There were the jade-green eyes but behind them there was no Narcissa. There was nobody. So if there was nobody in there I didn't kill anybody. Narcissa was not there. She escaped me. Always."

The room began buzzing with summertime and the walls shimmered as in a haze.

"Do you think you killed Narcissa Maidstone?"

"There never was any Narcissa. Never any real Narcissa." Only the lithe, willow-wand body, the jade eyes, the red lips, the red full luscious lips that said nothing and had always said nothing. The body was dead and he did not know who had killed it. Perhaps he had, and that was why he did not know, did not remember. A man who has nothing to fear, nothing to hide, has no need to throttle his memory....

Why was he saturated with this deep, pervasive stain of guilt? Why did he cry out, saying the blood is on my hands? Why did he feel that he had done it?

The eyes came back into view, and then there was the voice, coming to him as from a distance.

"Tell me everything in your own words."

"I've told you everything, Everything I could remember. And I think they were my own words."

There was the picture he had built up in himself of Narcissa, the image he had nurtured of Narcissa, shattered. And her moment of tenderness when she realized the picture was broken. She had kissed him then on the neck, a faint fairy kiss. There was the fairy kiss, and the darkness. And then later, much later—there was the lithe willow-wand body, the body never inhabited by a real Narcissa—lying spread across the smoky blue sofa, and where there should have been breath there was no breath, and where there should have been a light in the eyes there was no light. The lips, the full red lips, were popped agape in a little grimace of scorn and fear, and the tip of one breast, still and waxy as a gardenia with death, peeped out of the edge of a lavender blouse.

The flaxen hair was wound tightly around the white throat, and God had not said a word.

8

He ran into the hollyhocks, and a woman with a booming voice cried out, "Don't you try to hide from me!" And he said, "I didn't do it, Mom. Honest, I didn't do it."

But the razor strop was waiting for him, for Narcissa, like Porphyria, was dead.

"Do you understand that?" he said. "It was the razor strop. That's what I was afraid of. The razor strop. Do you understand that?"

"Yes," she said.

"But the other things I can't remember."

"The memories are never really gone," she said.

"No? Don't you think so?"

"Definitely not."

He sat up on the edge of the bed and looked across the green room toward her. There was the trace of a smile on her lips.

"I think you will work this out all right," she said. "Perhaps you are trying too hard."

And after a moment she was gone. How could he not try? He had to try. Everything depended on it.

But now he was caught up in the soft-gloved but merciless routine of the Whitman-Bourne Clinic, a hospital for the mentally disturbed. Every morning at seven he was awakened by Miss Dibble and a thermometer, and then began the ceaseless chatter of Dan Brian.

Brian was convinced that he was really cracked. He was really quite proud of it, and took pleasure in telling everyone all the details of his life. He alternated between excited volubility and extreme depression and spent hours, in defiance of the rules, lying on his bed in a kind of self-induced coma. He called this his "neurotic sleep."

Before breakfast everyone made his own bed, and at eight o'clock there was breakfast, and then at nine the garden. Everyone went to the garden, some because they liked to go and others because they were firmly persuaded to go. It was a formal garden which overlooked the East River, cut off from the world by high ornamental walls and delicate grillwork which, for all its grace, was solid steel and unshakable.

It was here, while deep in the intricacies of his own problem, that he met Helen. She was totally unlike that other Helen, about whose lovely ears the world crashed, and yet she too was pursued by her own fate, small but inscrutable.

It was summer, and they found themselves walking together.

"What do you do, Mr. Hanley," she asked, "to solace yourself in this vile and oppressive dungeon?"

"When I'm not thinking," he said, "which is most of the time—"

She interrupted with a little trill of flutelike laughter. "Ah, Mr. Hanley," she said, "you must not think. You really mustn't, you know."

"There is something I have to think about," he said.

"That's what's the matter with all of us," she said. "But go on, please. When you are not thinking, what do you do?"

He laughed because he was embarrassed. "Oh, nothing much," he said. "I guess I didn't tell you. I'm a cop."

"Oh? How exciting!"

"Not very. Cops don't do much of anything exciting."

She didn't reply and they walked once more around.

Then the nurses began gathering everyone together, and as they passed for the last time the leaden mass of the East River, Peter said, "I hope I will see you tomorrow."

"Yes. I'll be here tomorrow. Definitely I shall be here tomorrow."

And she gave him a quaint look and then they parted. She went to floor Eight, which was reserved exclusively for females who were not to be trusted with their own minds, bodies, or souls.

Everywhere the doors slammed shut. Shut and locked.

This was his life in a clinic for the mentally disturbed. Day faded into night and there was now no more sodium amytal, but up and down the corridors of his mind he searched for the answer to the question: What happened that night in Narcissa Maidstone's apartment?

Considering the deep burning rage in his own mind, certainly adequate motivation in itself, it would appear that he had done it, that with his hands he had strangled the life from that lithesome body. And yet the memories—the specific memories that he needed to produce—would not come. He desperately wanted them to come, and the desperation of his wanting them prevented their coming.

Then one day, when the August afternoon had gone into its savage midsummer festival dance, he was paid a visit by Inspector Battle, who sat in the green chair with his feet placed squarely before him and his hands holding his black hat on his knees.

"Nice place you have here," the inspector said.

"Just like the Harvard Club," Peter replied.

Inspector Battle picked up his hat, turned it

completely around, and put it down in his lap exactly as before.

"Do you remember the terrible time I had getting you in here?"

"Yes, a little. Tell me more about it."

"Well, in the first place the D.A. wanted you arrested. He still does."

"Yes, I knew that. What about the Commissioner?"

"It's hard sometimes to tell exactly what the Commissioner wants. At first I thought he wanted you hanged from the yardarm immediately."

"Why wasn't I?"

"Apparently he changed his mind. You see, there were some funny things about this case."

"I'll bet there were. How do they look now?"

Inspector Battle hesitated before speaking. "Quite a lot depends on you."

"What can I do?"

"I don't know exactly. What do you think you can do?"

Peter felt a sudden surge of rage—rage and frustration—and the words came boiling out like an overflowing volcano.

"How can I do anything? Here I am, confined in a madhouse, a spacious, luxurious, swank, plush and posh nuthouse! Ah, the corridors are wide and the rooms are trimmed in green, and you, Inspector Battle, sit on a maple chair and all this is like the Harvard Club, I am told over and over again. And all the doctors and nurses call me Mister and there are no straitjackets—at least, not yet. But the fact remains, Inspector, that this is a madhouse, and the windows are of steel and unbreakable glass and will not open the width of a man's body. And all the doors are locked. No doors will open anywhere!"

Inspector Battle took a short straight pipe out of his pocket, turned it over and over in his hamlike hands.

"I know all that, my boy," he said. "Don't you think we put you in here for a purpose?"

"Why? To keep me out of the hands of the D.A.?"

"More than that, son. We put you here to see if the doctors could help you remember."

"What do you want me to remember?"

"The facts. This was a murder case and you were in it. Deep in it. Things looked bad for you."

"Yes. I can imagine that."

"There was every indication"—and Inspector Battle's voice dropped to a professional confidential tone—"every indication that you did it."

"Do you think I did?"

The inspector looked away. But not before Peter had seen anxiety in those clear blue eyes.

"No, I don't think you did it. At least I hope you didn't. But we thought maybe sooner or later you could remember. When we found you, you could remember nothing. You were gabbling about St. Elmo's fire and somebody named Porphyria."

"That's the name of a girl in a poem by Robert Browning," Peter said. "I still remember the poem from school. It's about a girl who was strangled with her own hair."

"I see," said Inspector Battle. He was silent for a moment. Then he added, "That's not too good for you, either."

"What?"

"That you should remember that poem. It's a bit odd, the coincidence. She was strangled with her hair and you are gabbling about a girl in a poem who was strangled with her hair. I guess it doesn't mean anything, but do you often quote poetry? I don't remember your doing it. It doesn't seem like you."

"No," Peter said after a moment. "It isn't like me. I didn't realize I knew any poems. I guess I learned them better than I thought in school. Now—ever since this happened—they seem to be coming out.... Dr. Gatskill says it's probably caused by the trauma."

"The what?"

"The trauma. The shock. You never really forget anything, and so the things I learned in school could come out now."

"I see. Well, you weren't making much sense anyway."

"I still don't make sense."

"I can see that," said Inspector Battle.

Peter Hanley sat on the edge of his straight maple chair which stood beside a maple writing-desk. "Do you think I killed her?"

Inspector Battle fiddled with his squarish hat. He looked at the window where the drumfire of the boiling August tempest spattered and roared. Then he looked back at Peter.

"Do you think you killed her?"

Peter thought how easy it would be for him to say no. One little word that, if true, made all the difference between living in a nightmare and living in a world that was habitable. But the memories that would not come, and the significance of their not coming, had turned his every waking hour—even, he knew, his sleeping thoughts—into a nightmare world. His answer was an unknowing stare.

"Well, I don't," Inspector Battle said. "But the Chief of the Bureau thinks you killed her, and the Chief of the Department does, and so do the District Attorney and the Commissioner. And the Commissioner's man. Incidentally, I've got some bad news about him."

"Who? About whom?"

"The Commissioner's man. Scott."

"What's the story?"

"He's coming to see you."

"Oh."

"Well, I tried to prevent it. I didn't think it was a good idea, but what could I do?"

"You could have stopped him. He's not the Commissioner. Just a secretary."

Inspector Battle snorted. "A secretary who's held the job as long as he has always gets the backing of the office behind him."

"What does he want here?" Peter asked.

"Just wants to have a look for himself, I suppose."

"Well, let him snoop. What the hell do I care?"

"He'll be here today or tomorrow," said Inspector Battle.

"Makes no difference to me when George Scott wants to come."

Inspector Battle took out his pipe, thrust it into his pouch, loaded it, then put it back in his pocket. "Making any progress with your doctor?"

"Not much. She's given me the sodium amytal treatment twice but nothing happens."

"You can't remember?"

"Not enough to be worth anything."

"Do you remember seeing me?"

"When? I said good night to you in the Homicide Bureau."

"No. After that. In front of the Breakstone Apartments, on Park Avenue."

"I guess I remember it a little. Not much."

"You want me to tell you about it?"

"If you like."

"It might start you thinking on the right track."

"It might."

Inspector Battle told him about it.

When you've been in the business as long as Inspector Battle you get a kind of sixth sense. It tells you when trouble is around. And that night when Peter Hanley had said good night Inspector Battle knew that trouble was afoot. Not that it took a sixth sense for that. Not really.

"You had a haunted look in your eye, son. Do you know that?"

"Yes. I guess I did."

"And you were tired. Bone-tired and worn out. You never really got over the Julius Hassenpepper murder. Never got caught up on your sleep or anything."

"I guess you're right."

And, the inspector told him, after Peter had left the Homicide Bureau that night, Battle had sat back in the straight-backed chair in the austere office and, taking out his short squarish pipe, loaded it with pungent coarse tobacco and lighted up. He went over some old reports on the Hassenpepper case, not that there was anything new in them, or anything in particular that he was looking for, but Inspector Battle's life had been a study of death—violent death—and when he had a spare moment he liked to go over the old cases that he already knew in such intimate detail. Time passed pleasantly as the Inspector loaded and reloaded his pipe and pored through the reports on the case.

His telephone rang. The inspector put down the files of the case and answered it.

It was the rasping, nerve-racking voice of Chips Galligan of *The Daily Mail*.

"This Inspector Battle?"

"Yes."

"This is Chips. Chips Galligan."

"That's what I know."

"Do you know a cop named Hanley? He's supposed to be in your setup."

"Yes. I know him. He's in my bureau. What's happened?"

"Well, he's in some kind of a hassle in front of the Breakstone on Park Avenue."

"What kind of a hassle? Speak English."

"Looks like the law has the arm on the law, Inspector. A uniformed cop is holding him. I was riding around in a *Daily Mail* radio car with a cameraman when we got a tip from the City Desk."

"What's it all about?"

"Murder. Some babe. Looks like they figure your man did it."

Inspector Battle was already putting on his hat and buckling his pistol belt under his coat. "Do me a favor, Chips," he said.

"All right."

"Tell those coppers to stay right there. Don't let them take off for the station house."

"Well, I'll try, Inspector."

"Don't try. Do it."

Inspector Battle got a driver from the outer room and they took off, weaving through the traffic with the siren shrieking until they got uptown. At Sixty-seventh Street and Park Avenue they got out.

By the time he got inside the lobby of the Breakstone there were several detectives from the precinct there. Captain O'Hara was in a boiling mood.

"We've been hanging around here because of what the *Daily Mail* guy said," he complained: "Since when have you been issuing orders through newspaper reporters?"

"There wasn't time to do anything else," Inspector

Battle said. "What happened?"

"Your man here was wandering around on the street outside, talking gibberish. When the patrolman came along, Hanley took him up to Apartment 302 and there was a babe. Dead as a mackerel. Strangled. Her name was Narcissa Maidstone, as far as we know."

"So why do you think Lieutenant Hanley did it?"

"We don't think anything, Inspector. But he's been seeing a lot of this babe, and she's been playing around with other guys and he's off his rocker, so I guess it's a crime of passion."

"What do you mean he's off his rocker?"

"Well, when he come storming out of that place to get a cop he was talking way off the beam."

"You can be off the beam without committing crimes of passion," Inspector Battle observed. "Let me talk to him."

"All right," Captain O'Hara said in a peevish tone, "you talk to him. He's your man. It's your murder. Take it away."

O'Hara was right in one thing about Peter Hanley. He was considerably off the beam. But he had enough of his wits about him to recognize Inspector Battle.

"She escaped me," Hanley said. "She got away."

"Who got away?"

"St. Elmo's fire. The girl with the jade eyes."

"Talk sense, Peter."

"That's all the sense there is. That's the most sense I can think of. She got away, only she was never there. She was not there, so how could I do anything to her?"

"Do you think you did something to her?" Inspector Battle asked.

"No. But she's dead. I saw my love lying dead on a smoky blue sofa, and round her throat was wound her lovely flaxen hair. Like Porphyria, Inspector. Do you see? Like Porphyria."

Back at the Homicide Bureau, where there were only the two of them, Peter Hanley made no more sense than he had in the foyer of the Breakstone.

After a while Inspector Battle succeeded in getting hold of the Chief of the Bureau and the Chief agreed that, for the time being and the good of the service, it would be best to have Lieutenant Hanley in a psychiatric clinic. The matter went all the way up to the Commissioner's office, and the Commissioner also agreed, although with some reluctance. Perhaps it was not the best of all possible solutions, but it was something.

"I believed you were innocent," Battle said. "And I still do. But I have to admit there isn't much for me to base such a belief on."

Peter looked at him, and then around the room.

"I'm grateful for your faith," he said in a low tone. "If I could only remember more—"

"I talked to your doctor," said Inspector Battle, "and she assured me that memories never really disappear. With the right conditions, she tells me, you've got a good chance of coming up with just the memory that will untangle it all."

"I wish I could be sure of that," Peter said.

"There's nothing to be done but what we're doing."

Peter Hanley said nothing. He looked at the bleak but kindly eyes and then he looked out the window past the green curtains into the green treetops, and at the high arch of the Queensboro Bridge, and he saw the leaden scud in the sky and the dull mass of the structures on Welfare Island.

"Did it help any, for me to tell you what I knew?" Inspector Battle asked.

"No, but perhaps it will. Later."

"We won't be able to get away with this forever. Sooner or later they'll demand that you be let out of here. In fact, the D.A. is demanding that right now."

"So I understand."

"In the meantime we'll keep our fingers crossed and hope for the best."

When the inspector had gone Peter sat for a time trying to make the memories come, trying to make the jigsaw puzzle fall into shape, but there it was—an impenetrable barrier in his mind. It was almost a physical thing: he could feel its tightness across his forehead and desperately he felt that perhaps he could somehow seize it with his hands, tear it away with a crunching of bone and muscle, and then all would be well.

Dr. Gatskill poked her head in the door.

"How are you feeling?" she asked.

"All right."

"Not upset?"

"No. Why?"

"You never can tell about visitors," she said companionably. "Often they upset people. Sometimes the ones you think would upset them the least really upset them the most."

"They're traumatic, you mean?"

She grinned. "Now you leave the jargon to me. If you get yourself tangled up in jargon then you never will think your way out."

"Just think in my own words, you mean?"

"Yes. Just in your own words."

Suddenly he stood up, took a turn toward his bed, and then came around facing her.

"Doctor," he said, "I want you to tell me something."

"Yes?"

"Tell me one thing. Would surgery help?"

"What do you mean, would surgery help?"

"Would it help me to think? Would it help my brain?"

"There's nothing wrong with your brain, Lieutenant Hanley."

"But there's a wall there. I can really feel it. It's a kind of growth, I think—and it dams up the memories. The memories are behind it. I can feel the wall; it's made of muscle and bone; and if it could be cut out then I think I would be all right."

Dr. Gatskill gave him a long, penetrating look and then said, "There is a barrier, but it isn't physical. It can't be cut out with a knife."

"Then how can I get rid of it?"

"I think it will go away by itself. If you want some more jargon to amuse yourself with, it's called a psychic block. Perhaps there is something that you really don't want to remember."

"I want to remember everything!"

"Then just take it easy. Don't try too hard. Let it ride for a while. I think it will be all right without your straining."

Take it easy, Peter thought. Don't try too hard. So easy to say. But the doctor didn't know the D.A. or the Commissioner or the kind of life cops came in contact with. What was a repressed memory to them? They were hard-boiled men to whom psychiatry and psychotherapy seemed newfangled witchcraft. And suppose some newshawk—not cooperative like Chips Galligan—made a sensational story out of it. They could twist it every which way, put the heat on the big brass for action, and make a goat out of Peter, guilty or not guilty. And Dr. Gatskill was saying take it easy.

"I wish I could believe you."

"Do believe me. Please do believe me."

She went away, and he sat looking out the window

at the hot smoky day until Dan Brian and Milton DeBaer came in from playing badminton.

9

For her part, Dr. Gatskill was worried. She did not often worry about her patients, or allow any personal interest at all to come into the professional attitude. But the case of Peter Hanley was somehow different. She was not sure in quite what way it was different, but different it was.

She took the matter to her chief, Dr. Holmka. He received her in his little office, a twinkle of a smile in his eyes as she sat down and lighted a cigarette.

"What's on your mind, Doctor?"

Dr. Gatskill did not reply at once, but let her gaze wander from the tip of her cigarette to Dr. Holmka's face and then out the window to the river. When she spoke, it was quietly enough.

"I'm a little worried about Peter Hanley."

Dr. Holmka leaned forward slightly. "Worried? Worried in what way?"

Dr. Gatskill hesitated a moment. "This is not really a usual case, you know."

"Yes," said Dr. Holmka, "I know that. Besides being a patient, and in a state of shock, he is a murder suspect. Is that what you mean?"

"That's part of what I mean."

"What else?"

Dr. Gatskill hesitated another moment. Then she said, "I can't help thinking that Lieutenant Hanley is not altogether safe here."

Dr. Holmka gave her a curious look. "Not altogether safe? What do you mean by that?"

"Do you remember the time Professor Bolton made an attempt to kill him?"

"Yes," said Dr. Holmka. He made no comment and Dr. Gatskill did not expect him to. Dr. Holmka was not one to make many comments on matters of fact.

Dr. Gatskill looked at him carefully. "I can't help thinking but that was premeditated."

"Premeditated?"

"Yes. Oh, I know that Professor Bolton has a history of homicidal mania and he should not have been left alone on the floor—but still there was something rather peculiar about it."

"How was it peculiar?"

Dr. Gatskill put down her cigarette. "I don't know exactly. But I can't get over the idea that somehow it was prearranged."

"I suppose that is possible," said Dr. Holmka gravely. "Nearly everything is possible. But I'm afraid you are letting your imagination get the better of your professional judgment."

Dr. Gatskill, who had schooled herself to show no emotion, felt a slow red flush rise from the back of her neck and into her face. She saw, or thought she saw, that this had been noted by Dr. Holmka. He now had his gold pen out and was tapping it on the edge of his desk.

He said, "I think none of us can forget that we have human sensibilities, but at the same time we must not let them dominate us." He leaned forward slightly. "Just what exactly," he asked, "did you have in mind? Do you propose that we do anything specific?"

"I think it might be wise if we had a talk with Lieutenant Hanley's superiors one of these days soon. We might save ourselves—and them—and Lieutenant Hanley—quite a lot of trouble."

"Very well, we shall have a talk with them." He too rose as she turned to go.

Dr. Gatskill, instead of going back to her office, went straight to the fourth floor, where she found Peter Hanley alone in his room, reading a book.

"Hello, Doctor," he said. "What brings you here?" She gave him her quick professional smile.

"Just walking through," she said. "Thought I'd drop by and say hello."

Peter said, "I'm supposed to be in Occupational Therapy but I talked Miss Dibble out of it this time. I was getting pretty tired of that basketwork they had me doing. I don't think basket weaving is going to solve much of anything."

"Don't you?"

"No. I don't."

"Basket weaving relaxes the mind. In that way it helps to bring back the memories that need bringing back."

"It doesn't relax my mind," he said. "Just the opposite. Drives me nuts."

Dr. Gatskill gazed at him for a moment. Although he was a mature man, there was something boyish and perplexed in his eyes. And his cop's habitual hardness, which she knew better than most people to be chiefly pose, had fallen away and there was a look of naiveté about him.

Dr. Gatskill smiled slightly and turned to go. "Don't worry about it," she said, and went out into the corridor. Peter Hanley heard her footsteps echoing along the walls.

It was a thing he had to learn to live with. Other people had to live with jealousy, with resentment, with temper tantrums, with bad hearts and bad stomachs and bitter memories, but Peter Hanley had to learn to live with the idea that he could not find the truth. It would not come. The memories would not come.

He had to try to tell someone about it besides Dr. Gatskill—after all, she was a professional, and Peter, like the dwarf in the fairy tale, demanded something human.

He tried talking it out with Helen Parmelee while they made their interminable circles past the zinnias, past the asters, past all the golden summer flowers in the garden.

"You don't mind my telling you about these things, do you?" he asked.

"Why, no, sir," she said in her sweet way. "Why should I mind that? I am proud that you should tell me." Then, looking down at some of the plants, she added briskly, "Do you think that this trailing platypus gives fruits or berries? In its natural state, I mean."

He gave her a quick sharp look. Then he said, "I really wouldn't know. But I'm quite an admirer of these black-berried throckle trees."

She laughed slyly. "The summer-flowering glockenspiels are nice, too," she said.

Then he went over it all again; that is, the parts of his puzzle that he thought it proper for so sweet and so charmingly whacky a girl as she was to hear. When he came to the more dreadful parts, he did not go any further. There really was not much further to go anyway.

"You see?" he said. "The whole trouble is I can't remember the vital things."

"What a terrible woman that Narcissa was," Helen observed.

"Oh, no; not really terrible. Not at all terrible."

"She brought it all on herself."

"No. She really didn't. It was deeper than that."

But Helen made no reply, and they made two more turns around the garden before the nurses herded them all in groups according to their floors and led them to the big doorway.

"I have something to tell you, too," Helen whispered, just as they were about to part.

"What is it?"

"My doctor says that I will soon leave Eight, and then I will be on your floor. He thinks I'm safe enough to mix with the men now," she said. And she laughed her girlish little laugh.

"Congratulations," he said. "Sincerely. Congratulations."

She began to follow the other women from Eight inside. Then she looked back over her shoulder and said, "We must have something done about those pot-bellied Wheatena bushes."

"I'll borrow a pair of pinking shears," he said. "We'll make them all pink."

And everyone went upstairs, and the doors closed. All the doors closed.

10

Dr. Gatskill came to see him nearly every day and sometimes the interviews lasted an hour or so, but there was no more sodium amytal. She thought he had just better talk without drugs and see what came out. Nothing much did. Not at first, anyway. Later there were little intimations, and when they came, excitement came too, and the beginnings of real hope.

But this was not at first.

What there was at first was only the same

foundering of his own imagination—the things that surrounded the vital things.

Narcissa Maidstone had said very little to make him believe that he stood a ghost of a chance with her. What was there about her, then, and how did it happen that she appeared so suddenly on the stairway where he was investigating the tag end of a solved—or was it solved?—murder case. Was there really some connection? How could there be?

And yet he had been so dazzled by the jade-green eyes, by the cool voice that was like a distant waterfall in the mountains, that maybe he had not added up the whole score.

One thought, one pondered, one tried to decide—while the wailing wind of summer went by and autumn came in with a flick of gold in the windowpane—what was this thing called love? Now that it had gone, and love lay dead on a smoky blue sofa—how came all this to pass? What if it? What was it?

Love was a word that you tossed about like the thing they batted back and forth in a badminton game. Just a word. It meant something different to everyone. Certainly the love of a man for a woman was more than biology; it was perhaps a part of the ageless search for God. The woman was only the symbol, the idol of flesh and blood that stood for all the aspirations of the human heart. What a man wanted in a woman was not to be found in a woman. Not to be found anywhere at all, in heaven or in earth—except, possibly, in oneself. In the deep and hidden depths of one's own being.

But what nonsense was this he was thinking? The real thing he had to think out was all the circumstances of their meeting, all the little things that had escaped him because he was so bedazzled. He had to think out the details of their life together because in those details there might be the spark that would set the whole mind alight and—perhaps—turn him free. It was not freedom from Whitman-Bourne that he wanted—that, too, was only a symbol of a greater captivity—but freedom from the restraints of his own spirit.

One morning Miss Dibble came into the room with an air of repressed excitement. "You are not to go to the garden this morning," she said, "or to any other activities."

"No? Why?"

"You have a visitor coming to see you."

"Yes? Who is it?"

"The District Attorney."

"Well," said Peter with a wry grin, "I don't mind seeing the District Attorney. Just send him along."

"Oh," said Miss Dibble, "he isn't here yet. I'm just telling you not to go out."

"Well," said Peter, "I can wait for the District Attorney as long as he can wait for me."

"I expect you can," Miss Dibble said sharply and flounced out. Peter wondered for the thousandth time why she was allowed to work in a place where pleasant personality traits and an even temper were practically essentials. He guessed that it was deliberate; no doubt the authorities wished to test the reactions of the patients.

They want to see what comes out under pressure, Peter told himself, and he thought how many times, as a police officer, he had deliberately made people furious with him, for when they were furious their guard was down and sometimes they spoke the truth.

Peter told himself firmly that he was not nervous at meeting the District Attorney, and yet he found that there was a cold sticky sweat in the palms of his hands when at last the District Attorney arrived. He was preceded by Dr. Gatskill and followed by a couple of assistants, who were made to wait in the East Lounge, with the angelfish, the guppies, and the catfish.

Dr. Gatskill gave Peter a sharp and rather worried look, saying, "I've told Mr. Tummulty he can't have more than an hour. And be sure that you don't let yourself get worked up."

"What over?" Peter grinned. "Just because he wants to send me to the electric chair?"

Dr. Gatskill smiled grimly and went out, shutting the door behind her.

Peter, noting with a flicker of satisfaction that Dion Tummulty was already occupying the "patient's chair," seated himself on the edge of the bed, swinging his legs while he studied the District Attorney's face.

"I'm very sorry about all this," Tummulty said.

"I'm not too happy about it myself," Peter replied.

"Well, I didn't expect you to be happy. Now I hope you won't mind if I get right down to brass tacks."

"I wish you would."

The District Attorney shifted an immense briefcase on his knees. He was a pugnacious-looking man, with a continually outthrust jaw which suggested that he was always trying to convince himself of his own toughness. He was in the habit of displaying his courtroom mannerisms everywhere, even on purely social occasions, addressing everyone as though they were hostile witnesses. He was fired by political ambitions, and hoped to rise to the governorship. Peter knew he was a dangerous man to have as an opponent.

"I want to be frank with you," Tummulty said. "I

realize you've been a police officer with a first-class record and that you're a man of exceptional intelligence. This is all the more noteworthy in a department not exactly celebrated for its intelligence."

His jaw snapped shut, as it invariably did at the end of a sentence, and Peter said, "Thanks."

"All this must make it difficult for you," Tummulty said. "However, I said I was going to be frank and I am. The fact is, I'm not fooled for a minute by the strategy of your department in putting you in this place."

"Is it strategy?" said Peter.

"Of course it's strategy!" the District Attorney snorted. "Your chief knew that the best thing to do with you was get you quietly out of the way."

"Don't you think it's possible," said Peter, "that my chief is trying to do exactly what he says he's doing? Which is to get at the truth?"

"Nonsense! How could anyone get at the truth in a place like this?"

"There are a lot of things I can't remember," said Peter.

Tummulty leaned forward and peered intently at him, saying, "You could remember them if you wanted to."

"Are you suggesting I'm deliberately concealing the facts?"

The District Attorney leaned even farther forward on the edge of the maple chair.

"That is exactly what I am suggesting."

"Then why did you come here?" Peter asked.

"I came here to save us the bother of going to trial."

"You don't want to save the bother of a trial," Peter said. "You would prefer having a trial, wouldn't you? It would make a good case for you."

The District Attorney clutched his briefcase more tightly than ever. An angry gleam came into his eyes.

"Look here!" he exclaimed. "You're not in a position to question my motives. You're already in a bad spot and I can put you in a worse one if I want to. I can get a writ of habeas corpus and have you in jail in no more time than it takes me to get to the Criminal Courts."

"All right," said Peter. "What do you want me to do?"

"I want you to do the simplest thing in the world. I want you to tell the truth."

"I'll be glad to do that," Peter said. "That is, as far as I can go."

"Would you be willing to answer my questions?"

"As far as I can go," Peter replied. "What do you want me to answer?"

Dion Tummulty shifted slightly in his seat, cocking his head to one side. There was a little gleam in his small eyes.

"How long did you know Narcissa Maidstone?" he asked.

"About a year," replied Peter. "Maybe a little more."

Tummulty nodded curtly, to indicate that this checked with his own findings.

"How well did you know her?"

"Pretty well."

"How well? Speaking acquaintance? Take her to the theater? Sleep with her? Or what?"

Peter looked at the window for a long moment. "Slept with her," he said slowly.

"Ah!" Tummulty emitted a sharp breath. "You slept with her! Was this a regular arrangement? A permanent one, I mean?"

Peter brought his eyes back. "Scarcely permanent," he said. "She's dead."

"I don't think your trivial remarks will improve matters," Tummulty snapped.

"All right. Go ahead with the questions."

"Very well. How long had your relations with Narcissa Maidstone been intimate?"

"About six months, I suppose."

"Were they satisfactory?"

"What's that got to do with it? Aren't you getting a little off the track, Mr. Tummulty?"

"Not at all."

"I'd like you to explain just what you meant by that question."

"All right. I'll explain. It's a question of motive, Lieutenant Hanley."

"What makes you think there's any motive at all?"

"Now look, Hanley. If you prefer, I'll ask these questions in court, and we'll stop right here." His jaw snapped shut sharply.

"All right," Peter said. "Go on."

"I asked you if your intimate relations with Narcissa Maidstone were satisfactory."

"No, to be frank, they weren't."

"Why not?"

"I don't think she was especially interested in me."

"Physically—or as a person?"

"Both."

"Ah!"

"You sound satisfied. Is that the answer you were looking for?"

"I want to ask you one more thing. Did you know that Narcissa Maidstone had a good many lovers besides you?"

"I suspected it."

"When did you begin to suspect it?"

"Quite a while ago."

"How did that make you feel?"

"What do you mean how did it make me feel?"

"Angry? Depressed? What?"

"Angry, I guess."

"Angry, you guess. You were furious, weren't you?"

"I don't know. I suppose so."

"And on the evening that you were brought here—the evening that Narcissa Maidstone was killed—you were in a rage, a rage of jealousy and frustration, were you not? That evening you went to Narcissa Maidstone's apartment to have it out with her, didn't you?"

Peter Hanley got up off the edge of the bed, walked to the window, looked out, and then turned toward the center of the room. The District Attorney was watching him closely.

"Well?" he said. "That's not a very hard question. You were furious and you went to her apartment to have it out, didn't you?"

"Yes. I was furious. But that's all I remember. I don't remember going to her apartment."

Dion Tummulty leaned back, a faint intimation of amiability spreading over his face.

Peter went on: "What you want me to say now is that I had an argument with her, a fight, and during it I choked her to death. That's what you think happened and that's what you want me to say. Isn't it?"

The District Attorney leaned back and folded his arms. The briefcase balanced itself neatly on his knees. "Well, isn't that what happened?"

Peter sat down on the edge of the bed again. "Mr. Tummulty," he said, "I don't know what happened. I really don't know. I know they found me outside her apartment. But I don't think I killed her."

"Who do you think did kill her?"

"I don't know that either."

The District Attorney took up his briefcase and rose. His jaw was relaxed and there was a self-satisfied look on his face.

"I don't think any more questions are necessary, Lieutenant Hanley. And really, I must say, as a police officer you ought to be able to see that this case is open and shut. Open and shut, Lieutenant Hanley. Good-by."

He strode with a self-assured little swagger out of the room and, joined in the corridor by his assistants, headed his little procession as it marched off toward the elevators.

After a while Dr. Gatskill put her head in the door. "What luck?" she asked.

"He's after my scalp. Looks like he might get it, too." She stood silent for a moment.

"He hasn't got it yet," she observed. Then she was gone.

11

Come to think of it, it was rather a dizzy crowd Narcissa traveled in. He had never thought much about the crowd, but now he did. She was a singer, and that accounted for a lot. Nightclub singers had nearly as screwball a lot of acquaintances as coppers.

After the first evening in her apartment, on that smoky blue sofa, when she told him her problem—what was that problem now?—he was naturally interested in what she did for a living. He asked her point-blank.

She gave him a look with the long lazy green eyes.

"What did you think I did?"

"I didn't know. I just asked."

"Something not quite nice?"

"Please don't be unpleasant," he said. "It. was just a question. It doesn't matter."

"I'm not particularly complimented by the fact that you don't recognize me."

"I'm sorry," he said. "Should I?"

"I'm called Narcissa," she said.

"Yes?"

"Narcissa. I was at the Leopard Room for a solid year. I have been at the Crown Club for the last six months. Did you never hear of Narcissa, copper?"

She gave him an intense look, one filled with concern. The thought flashed through his mind: What is this girl frightened of? Failure? But that was incredible.

"Oh, you're *that* Narcissa."

"Yes," she said. "*That* Narcissa."

"I heard you sing when you were at the Leopard Room. You sang some popular songs and then you sang a couple of French ones. "Les Yeux du Soir" was the name of one of them."

Her face lighted up, the jade eyes flashed. "You remember?"

"Yes, I remember."

"But you didn't remember me. You didn't remember I was the same Narcissa."

"You are a lot different on the stage."

"Better—or worse?"

For a policeman he was an adroit man. "Oh, different. You have a stage personality and you have a real personality. They're not the same."

She thought about this for a minute and then she said, "What were you doing in the Leopard Room, anyhow?"

"That's an odd question. Why shouldn't I be in the Leopard Room? You mean it's a funny place for a copper to be?"

"Well, sort of."

"As a matter of fact," he said, "I was there that time on a job. It was a little different from the usual job—" He remembered well enough what it was; it was the time General Joselito San Blas was up from the south, and the Bureau had a request to keep a watch on him. The local patriots were anxious to blot General Joselito San Blas out of the picture, and the State Department put the bite on New York's Finest to see that the General was not blotted out of the picture while he was in their town. As a matter of fact, on the way home he had a mysterious accident: he fell out of the plane door into the blue Caribbean Sea. But all that had nothing to do with Narcissa, so he didn't bother to tell her about it.

"Anything you care to tell me about?" she said.

"No—just one of those things. But I don't want you to get the idea that I wouldn't be in the Leopard Room just for fun. I like to get around like anybody else. I guess you think of all cops as flatfeet who never got out of the second grade. As a matter of fact I went to NYU and on top of that I took a law degree. Does that impress you?"

"Very much," she said.

"When I was in school I wrote little plays for the Drama Society and I also acted in them. My first play was about a Chinese, in some indefinite ancient period, who murdered his wife, whom he greatly adored, as a sacrifice to his honor. I forget exactly what the point of honor was."

"And from that you went to the Homicide Bureau."

Peter smiled faintly. "Not quite that directly. Do you

really think there is a connection?"

"Could be," she said.

"You're too deep."

"I'm not very deep. But that was a point, wasn't it?"

"Yes. I guess there was a point. All this fit your picture of a copper?"

"I didn't have a picture of a copper."

"Oh, yes, you did. Everybody has a picture of everything."

"Now it's you who are being deep. What's your picture of me?"

What was his picture of her? He couldn't say, couldn't tell her, couldn't tell himself. The picture you make does not necessarily coincide with the reality, or to put it another way, the only reality is in the picture you make. As the metaphysical tinkers said, when a tree falls in a forest, there is no sound if there is no ear around to hear it. The sound is in the mind of him who hears ...

"Come to think of it, I don't have any picture of you either," he said. "I just like to look at you. You are cool and beautiful."

She said nothing at first, and when she did her voice was very low and almost humble; for her, that is, almost humble. "That is a very wonderful thing to say."

"Once upon a time," he said, "I was in the Army and I was in a place called Fort Missoula, Montana. That's a long way away from here, and to me, a New York kid, it seemed a long way away from anywhere. I used to look out the barracks window to the south, and there was a mountain top, Mount LoLo it was called, and it was near there that an Indian princess led the explorers, Lewis and Clark, through a mountain pass to safety. Well, I used to sit at the barracks window, and there was that mountain top, Mount LoLo, white and infinitely pure and remote and cool and unattainable. It was a symbol, I guess—all the things I ever wanted, all the things that were out of reach. You are like Mount LoLo a little …"

She sat without speaking, twisting the edge of a playing card. It was the Knave of Hearts.

"You're crying," he said. "What are you crying for?"

"I don't know," she said.

"Life is really not so wonderful as I have been led to believe," he said.

"What do you mean by that?"

It was a hot Sunday afternoon and they were sitting at an outdoor café on Park Avenue called, incredibly enough, Le Rêve. It was supposed to be like Paris, but there is nothing about Park Avenue that is even remotely like Paris. It just isn't the same thing. But outside of France he knew of only two sidewalk cafés: one in London and one in New York. This one.

Narcissa was sipping an apéritif called quinquina because this, Peter assured her, was truly Parisian, and she said she wanted to do something that was truly Parisian. She had never been in Paris, and he, for his part, had never seen or heard of quinquina in America; and the last time he had had any he was sitting under an awning of the Café de la Paix, and the waiter, speaking to him in a combination of French, German, and English, explained in great detail what quinquina was.

"Quinine," the waiter wound up. "It's the same thing as quinine."

"Oh, I see," said Peter. "Why didn't you say so in the first place? When you say it in French it comes out *can-kee-na*, and that doesn't sound like quinine a bit."

But that was 1944 or 1945, when Peter was a captain

in the CID at the MP headquarters in Pigalle, and this was 1951 and a café on Park Avenue called Le Rêve and he was talking about something else altogether. "Is life just what you had been led to believe?"

She put down the quinquina and gave him an enigmatic look. "I was never led to believe anything. So I guess it turned out all right for me. What about you?"

"I don't know precisely. But I always expected something different. I was always looking for something that wasn't there."

She was watching a girl crossing the street and her eyes were full of the other girl's costume. But she said, "Tell me about it."

"Let's put it this way. On a wonderful day in June I go to the beach. The sunshine is extra special, it pours over you like champagne. I get into my swimming shorts and stretch out in a nice easy chair and everything is wonderful; it's perfect. And yet it isn't wonderful enough. I want something else. Better sunshine. I'm looking for some kind of sunshine that isn't there. Doesn't exist."

"I don't get it," she said, and now she was watching a young man in a broad-shouldered pinstripe suit.

"I didn't think you would," he said. "I don't think you even heard me."

"Yes, I heard you," she said. "Tell me something, copper. Does going to bed do it? Does that give you what you want?"

"Going to bed?"

"With a girl, I mean. Is that good enough for you?"

He thought about that for a minute.

"I see what you mean," he said. "Well, that is very good. It's about the best, I guess. But, to answer your question, no. It isn't good enough. I always want it to be something better, and, when it's happened, it's over, there isn't anything at all. Nothing."

She began turning the flare-edge apéritif glass round and round on the checked tablecloth. "Sometimes," she said, staring into the glass, "sometimes I don't like you too much."

"I thought you might say that," he said.

She drank the last of the quinquina, and smoothed her summery dress with her long cool fingers.

12

There was no more sodium amytal, but Dr. Gatskill was always asking questions. She was a kind of female Dr. Ink-Blot herself. She would ask him a very general question and then she would expect Peter to carry on from there. Dr. Ink-Blot himself—that is, Dr. Fredric Holmka—had this technique down to a fiendish perfection. He would ask you how you felt, or how you liked the weather, but he would ask it with such a feeling of intensity you would think you had to say something pretty important, and you would end up telling him some terrific stuff, such as, maybe, how all your life you'd wanted to cut your grandmother's heart out with a paring knife, or something like that. Dr. Ink-Blot was so named because his amorphous questions were like the inkblot test that some psychiatrists were said to use: you got out of the shapes, not what was in them, but what was in your own mind.

Dr. Gatskill used the conversational inkblot method with a little more moderation, a little less intensity. She would ask the general questions, but not in quite the same way.

And Peter would say, "I don't understand just what you want to know."

"Don't try to be specific," she would reply. "Say whatever comes into your head. Just wander."

So he would wander, and in this way some things would come out that often were a great surprise to him.

One day she said, "Tell me about this person Narcissa. What was she like? What did you think of her? Start by telling me how she looked."

When he tried to describe Narcissa, he found it difficult. Almost impossible. What he remembered was the jade-green eyes, the slim lithe figure, the smooth complexion, and the flaxen hair.

"She was tall, I think," he said. "Taller than most. And she had a way of looking at you—it was remote, it told you to go away and to come, both at the same time. Do you understand that?"

"Yes. Go on. What was she like? How did she look?"

"I don't know, really," he said after some thought. "I find it hard to remember."

"Why?"

Always that insistent question—why? Why this? Why that? How could you answer *Why* to every question in life? The question came back at him.

"Why? Don't you know why you find it hard to remember?"

Well, he didn't see her very clearly. He had a picture in his mind, only it was not really a picture, it was a symbol; when he saw Narcissa, it was the symbol he saw, not Narcissa.

"But that doesn't make sense," he said.

"I think it makes a lot of sense," said Dr. Gatskill. "Tell me about the symbol. What was that like?"

He thought about that. What was the symbol like? What was it that he saw there? But the answers wouldn't come.

"Why were you, attracted to her?" Dr. Gatskill asked.

"That is the sixty-four-dollar question."

He began to think about Narcissa. More and more about the elusive, flaxen-haired Narcissa. In the deep, tortuous labyrinths of his mind there were memories he wanted to bring back, memories that might save him, if not from Dion Tummulty, then at least from himself; but always he had the feeling of running down dark hallways and beating on closed doors and crying, "Open! Let me in! Open the doors!"

He tried to think what Narcissa was like, but at last he gave it up. He did not really know. But it was an odd crowd that she ran with, and he thought about that.

There was Cal Sharkey, for instance. A more peculiar sort of person Peter had never seen, and just where Cal fitted into Narcissa's bright-colored patchwork picture he did not quite know—except that Sharkey was a press agent, and Narcissa had a faith in press agents such as other people have in incantations and herbal brews.

He first saw Cal Sharkey in the Alhambra Room—that dimly lit place in Manhattan where so much of his life had gone—which had become, indeed, the setting for the passion which swept him. It was a dark and airless little place at best, its trimmings and decorations all in Moorish style, and there, at three o'clock or perhaps it was four o'clock in the morning, was Cal Sharkey. Peter and Narcissa were at a table in a far corner, isolated from the sea of people, from the noise, the hammering and beating of life, the fake and faded gaiety. The little man appeared out of the smoke. Narcissa introduced him.

"This is Cal Sharkey," she said. "Sit down, Cal. What are you drinking?"

Cal sat down and he was drinking Old Crow. One hundred proof Old Crow, and he took it neat. Strong medicine for such a frail little man, Peter thought. Well, you never could tell ...

"Who is Cal Sharkey?" Peter asked, with no cordiality whatever.

Narcissa caught the tone and tossed it back to him, unpleasantly. "One of my friends," she said. "Any objections?"

"Not specifically."

Sharkey paid no attention, and tossed off another whisky.

Narcissa's tone softened. "Cal Sharkey," she said, "is my mentor. If it weren't for him, I wouldn't be where I am today."

"Where are you today?"

She ignored it.

"Mr. Sharkey," she said, "has brought me what little success I've had. By the power of the printed word. You ought to know what that means, copper. It seems to have had something to do with your success as well. You could conceivably be walking a beat in Staten Island, I suppose ..."

Yes, he could be.

Cal Sharkey was sipping his drink. He stopped, ran his hands through his straight black hair.

"Your friend's a copper, Cissy?" he asked.

"Yes."

Sharkey finished his drink. "You pick up some odd bric-a-brac," he observed.

"Including you?" Peter asked.

"Now, please," said Narcissa. "You boys mustn't quarrel. I don't want any quarreling."

"How can I quarrel?" said Sharkey. "I don't even know the guy."

After that they established some kind of a *modus vivendi*, as the diplomats put it, and after a couple of drinks Peter got so he could tolerate the man, but just barely.

Sharkey had three neat ones, none of which he paid for, and when nobody offered him another he got up and left. He didn't even say good night.

"Odd kind of fish, that one," Peter remarked. "If he were around on a homicide case, he'd be the first one I'd pick up."

"Why?"

"The little quiet guys are always packed with dynamite. Look out for the guys who never say much."

"You're quite a psychologist, aren't you?"

"Not so you could notice it," he said.

Well, that was the kind of thing she was surrounded with. Cal Sharkey was only one of many. There were musicians, entertainers, columnists, taxi drivers, and assorted characters of no particular occupation. No women. Just men. Must be something in her ego that demanded she be surrounded by a circle of men. She didn't necessarily like them, or want to know them very well. She just wanted them there. They gave her some kind of a feeling of security.

Soon after Cal Sharkey went, they decided to go. That was the first time he kissed her. That night. Not there, in the Alhambra Room, but later.

They had taken a taxi and were riding in the austere nocturnal beauty of Park Avenue, and what surprised him was the quality of her kiss. A kiss has a quality; it is a physical thing, lips meeting lips, and yet it has another quality, too. Of the spirit, no doubt. What surprised him about the quality of her kiss was its delicacy, its remoteness. It lingered like honey, and yet it was far-off and unreal. That surprised him then. Later it infuriated him.

She was elusive, not really there.

Now, trying to remember under the persistent questioning of Dr. Gatskill, while August changed her dress and became September, he saw that it was this, this elusiveness, which charmed him, fascinated him, and nearly drove him mad.

Perhaps it had truly driven him mad.

There were other queer fish.

One day he ran into Narcissa on Fifth Avenue, walking in a shimmering dress in the shimmering sunlight, and she was with a man known as Crowfoot Lance. Crowfoot Lance was a disbarred lawyer, and Peter knew that he had been something in the Julius Hassenpepper setup. Had been and no doubt still was, in whatever was left of the Hassenpepper setup. In the police investigation they had never been able to bring out precisely what Lance was, but they surmised that he was a sort of legal adviser to the boss. It wasn't too clear.

Well, there was Narcissa walking along Fifth Avenue with Crowfoot Lance, and at the time it did not seem to have too much meaning: Narcissa knew such an odd lot of characters that one more didn't seem to matter, but now he wondered. Perhaps it did matter.

She had said, "Peter, this is Mr. Lance. He and I have been friends for many years."

"Yes," Peter replied. "I've known Mr. Lance for a long time. That is, in a way."

"Oh, that's very nice," Narcissa said.

"Not so nice," said Peter.

"Now don't be awkward," Narcissa said.

He walked half a block along Fifth Avenue with them—and when they got to the corner opposite St. Patrick's he said good-by. And now he wondered, as he had not seemed to wonder before, just where Crowfoot Lance belonged in this picture. Why should Narcissa have known Lance?

"If I could only remember a few more things," he said slowly. "There is so much that I can't remember."

"Do you think," Dr. Gatskill said, "it would help any if you went back—if you left here?"

"I don't know," he said. "Besides, if I got out of here, the Commissioner would turn me over to the D.A. and the D.A. would have me in jail in five minutes."

"It might be arranged with Inspector Battle," Dr. Gatskill said, "to let you go back for only a little while."

He looked out the window, knowing that the answers weren't out there at all, but here, in him, in his own mind, and he said, "I don't think it would do any good for me to leave. Not yet anyway."

"It's all up to you," she said. "We try to help but in the long run, only you can solve your problem."

"Yes, I know that."

She left, and he sat staring at the dusty treetops and the faded sky. Then he got up and walked into the East Lounge, where he toyed with a red pawn of the chess set as he looked down on a tug churning against the tide. Usually they managed to arrange their comings and goings with the tide, but this one was doing things the hard way. He sighed. He guessed that was what he was doing: churning against the tide. He put down the pawn and began walking up and down the corridor.

13

Helen Parmelee arrived on the floor from Eight. It was an occasion and everyone congratulated her. When you got off one of the "bad floors" onto a good one everyone congratulated you. The arrangement on Four was that one wing was for women, the other for men, and the two sexes mingled at mealtimes and in the central "common lounge." This was considered a good idea for their recovery, because a lot of the men were suffering from woman trouble of one kind or another, and among the women there were those who had man trouble.

"It all goes back to their fathers and mothers," said Brian, who exuded more technical psychiatric information than any of the staff psychiatrists.

"Does it?" Peter asked.

"Yes. All subconscious, you know. Now me, I have father trouble. My father is the most traumatic person in the whole world."

"Traumatic?"

Brian snapped his fingers impatiently. "Traumatic. Trauma. Medical term for shock."

"Is your father shocking?"

"Well, you know what I mean."

The dining room was on the north side. It contained six tables with four places each. The atmosphere, as in the rest of the Whitman-Bourne Clinic, was one of clubby informality.

"I feel shy," Helen said.

"Do you? Why?" Peter asked.

"Well, when I was on Eight there were all women. There wasn't much freedom. Now, with a little freedom, I feel shy."

"How do you feel otherwise?"

"Oh, fine otherwise. How about you?"

"Oh, I'm all right in a general way." And Peter thought about how in this clinic you didn't have to be a doctor to tell how people really were inside. You could find out with the simple question: "How are you?" The very sick ones were so depressed by this question that they could not answer at all, but just looked at you with infinite melancholy and resentment. Those next in line wanted to tell you in detail all the things that were wrong with them. And those who were nearly well just said they were fine. But those who were about to leave said, "Fine, thanks, how are you?"

But this was going off on a tangent, thinking along these lines. He was here for a purpose. He was here to untangle some memories—from a trauma, as Brian would have said—and his troubles were not deep-lying but, again as Brian would have said, "situational." His loss of memory was caused by the situation, not by something far back and inherent in the intricate patterns of his childhood and the rest of his life.

Or was it?

The following morning there was a thunderstorm. It woke everyone at half past six and lasted for nearly an hour. The flashes of lightning lit up all the walls and then the thunder roared as though the roof were coming down. The rain came in sheets and Peter stood beside his window watching with Milt DeBaer. Dan Brian was in his bed with the sheet over his head.

After the thunderstorm was over Miss Dibble came in and in her crisp official voice said, "Please don't go to the garden this morning, Mr. Hanley."

He had counted on his usual walk with Helen and he was not only disappointed but resentful. He wondered if the chart writers had done this. Maybe they had written so much about that walk in the corridor the previous night that the doctors had decided to cut down his time with Helen.

"Why can't I go to the garden?" he asked.

Miss Dibble laughed in rather a pained way. "You surprise me, Mr. Hanley. Most of you people want to get out of the routine. But it's nothing permanent, you can go to the garden tomorrow. And every day after. This morning Dr. Holmka wants to see you at nine-thirty. Please be in your room."

Peter lounged in the easy chair and waited.

At nine-thirty Dr. Holmka came in with Dr. Gatskill. Dr. Holmka was a compact person, rather swarthy in complexion, and with a piercing eye. There was a courtly and old-worldly manner about him. He was in fact a Viennese with Swedish in his blood. He had the coloring of Southern Europe but his eyes were of the Far North. They were blue as the fjords, and this effect was curious and impressive.

Dr. Holmka leaned forward slightly in his chair and said, "How are you?" He managed to put an air of intensity into that simple question. It was very uncomfortable, and it was meant to be. He waited expectantly, as though something portentous hung in the balance.

"Oh!" Peter said. "I'm all right."

Dr. Holmka's sharp tone leaped across the room's quietness. "All right? What do you mean when you say 'all right'?"

"Why, just what everyone means," Peter said rather angrily. "Doesn't it mean the same thing to everyone?"

"Oh, by no means!" said Dr. Holmka. "Some people say it when they're really feeling dreadful and they want to cover up. Are you the kind of person who tells himself he is feeling fine when he's really feeling dreadful?"

"No," Peter said, "I'm not that kind."

Dr. Holmka toyed for a moment with a thick gold fountain pen. "Are you worried? Anxious?"

"No," said Peter.

"Do you feel depressed?"

"No."

"Elated, then?"

"No. I just feel all right."

"No feelings of anxiety?"

"No."

Dr. Holmka was silent for another moment. Dr. Gatskill, who had been sitting on the edge of the bed with her eyes fixed on Peter, folded her hands. Then Dr. Holmka said, "You have every reason to feel anxiety. It would be strange if you did not."

"Why?"

A little smile, like the ripple of a breeze lost from the Danube, came upon the ice-blue fjords.

"Let us recapitulate," he said, "and see what your situation really is. You are a New York City detective. Is that right?"

Peter grinned. "Right so far," he said.

"And you are suspected—at least you are in a position to be suspected—of a murder. The murder of a beautiful girl. Is that also right so far?"

Peter felt a vise tighten about his forehead and he saw that Dr. Holmka was watching him, that Dr. Holmka saw every tiny change in expression, every shade of mood, of suppressed emotion.

"Yes. Right so far."

"Then," Dr. Holmka said with the crispness of a surgeon pointing to a tumor uncovered by the scalpel, "do you not think there is something in your position that might cause a man anxiety? A normal man, I mean."

Peter felt a hot flush on his face. "I am a normal man, Doctor. Are you trying to say that I'm not?"

"Oh, no, not a bit. I'm only saying that a normal man, in your position, would feel some anxiety."

Peter clenched his fists and unclenched them. The room's silence became oppressive.

"Yes," he said with a suppressed fury. "Yes. I feel worried. I do feel worried. There's no getting around that."

Dr. Holmka leaned forward a little more and, tapping his thick gold pen on his knee, said, "Just exactly what is it you are worried about?"

Peter looked at him with surprise. "You've just told me what it is that I'm worried about. You said it was enough for any normal man—"

Dr. Holmka shifted his position and his tone, both very slightly. "Yes, I know, but what I'm asking now is just what it is. What specific thing in your present situation makes you anxious? What—specifically?"

Peter thought for a while. It seemed to him that the whole general picture was quite enough to have on his mind. But then he said, "I suppose it's not knowing just what happened. Not being able to remember."

The doctor's eyes flashed and drove at him like rapiers. "You mean you're afraid you might have killed this girl yourself?"

It was a cruel, bold, naked question. Peter was not prepared for it. The question stood in the room like a figure in scarlet, stood and pointed a long naked finger at him. Did he, Peter Hanley, kill the girl, the girl

Narcissa Maidstone? Did he?

"Yes," Peter said. "That's what worries me. I guess that's it. It's hard to think about."

"Do you think you find it all so unpleasant that you can't think straight about it?"

"Perhaps."

"Do you think that trying so hard to remember prevents you from remembering?"

"Could be."

Dr. Holmka was tapping the gold pen on his knee.

"This is perhaps what we sometimes call a psychic block. The memory is so unacceptable—so unpleasant—that we cannot face it. We bury it deeply. But I do not intend to burden you with details of that kind. You will find your way out of your troubles in your own way. But"—he held the pen pointed in the air—"we might be able to help you a little more than we have yet been able to. You want us to help you, don't you, Mr. Hanley? It is important that you want us to help."

"Yes!" Peter let the answer burst forth like an explosion. "Yes! I want all the help I can get!"

Dr. Holmka looked briefly at Dr. Gatskill and then he looked back again. "There are various kinds of therapy. There is of course the most important of all, the psychotherapy—the interviews—in which Dr. Gatskill and I have tried to help you. Do you feel that you have been helped?"

"A little," Peter said. "Not much. I feel a little better about things, but still I don't feel that I'm getting any closer to the solution. I'm not getting the memories."

"There are other forms of therapy which might help you," Dr. Holmka continued. "For example, deep shock—electroshock. But we do not feel that this treatment is applicable to your case. There is also subshock, or insulin shock. But we believe that this also is not necessary."

He paused a moment and Peter waited for what was to come.

"You will recall," Dr. Holmka said, "that when you were first here we gave you a drug called sodium amytal. Do you know what the purpose of that was?"

"To make me talk," said Peter.

"Exactly. The drug acts a bit like alcohol, but it is easier to control. It relaxes and tends to cut out the inhibitory centers of the mind. Thus the truth is more likely to come out."

"*In vino veritas*," said Peter.

"Yes," said Dr. Holmka with his gracious little smile, "in wine there is truth."

"But I didn't get much of anywhere with the sodium amytal," said Peter.

"No, we didn't get much out of you. But what we propose to do now is to try it again—more extensively. We will keep you under for a much longer time. About forty-eight hours. Would you have any objection?"

"Objection? Why should I have?"

Dr. Holmka looked at him very intently. "Some people," he said, "are quite fearful of what they might say when their guard is down. Are you fearful?"

"No."

No, he said—his voice said no—but he was not sure. "In any case," he said grimly, "we must know the truth. I must know the truth."

"Then," Dr. Holmka said, "with your permission, we will put you under this treatment next week." He got up, gave his courtly little mid-European bow, and said to Dr. Gatskill, "Please ask Miss Dibble to have him moved to a private room before Monday."

Dr. Holmka then shook Peter's hand with a single

short decisive motion and he and Dr. Gatskill went off down the corridor. Peter heard his low voice, speaking rapidly and intently to Dr. Gatskill. Then the silence of the fourth floor settled down until everyone came back from the garden.

Dan Brian came in with a bit of paper folded into a neat small square.

"A young lady in the garden sent this to you."

"Thanks."

Peter opened it up. It said: *I missed you.*

There was a faint old-fashioned perfume about the note. He thought it was lilac.

14

The next day George Scott came to see him. He was brought in by Miss Dibble, who shut the door and left.

"Well, Lieutenant," said Scott, "how are you feeling?" He sat down without waiting for an invitation, in the green-covered maple chair. Peter did not sit, but walked back and forth, resting occasionally against the writing desk. Scott fixed his small but rather kindly eyes on him, watching him all the time.

"I'm feeling all right," said Peter. "How about you?"

"Oh, you know, up and down. Pretty good. The Commissioner thought somebody had better see you. I guess he didn't think it was very important, so he sent me."

"Yes?"

Scott gave a little chuckle. "Well, you understand what I mean. I'm just his secretary, kind of an errand boy. If he'd thought it was important he'd have come himself."

"Yes, of course."

Peter took another turn from the writing table to the door and back. Scott watched him all the time.

"You know," he said, "the Commissioner was pretty upset by all this."

"I can imagine."

"He wanted you tried right away. For the good of the Department."

"Well, why didn't he do it?"

"I talked him out of it."

"You did? Why?"

"Partly because Inspector Battle was so anxious not to have you tried. I like to help keep the Department happy. That's one of my jobs, as I see it. Kind of a liaison between the Commissioner and the men in the line. Also, I didn't think it was fair for you to go into court in your condition."

"What did you know about my condition?"

"Well, I saw the reports. I didn't think it was fair for you to stand a trial."

"That was nice of you."

"You were pretty irrational," said George Scott. "It seemed to me the best thing for you was to be in a place like this. For a while, anyway. Until they found out just what ailed you."

"Yes?"

Scott leaned forward slightly. "Lieutenant Hanley, do you remember ever having seen me before?"

Peter stared at him. "Of course I do. At the Commissioner's office a couple of times, and around the Homicide Bureau once or twice, I guess."

"No other time?"

"Not that I know of."

"You don't remember having seen me the night all this happened?"

"No."

"I was in the Homicide Bureau for a while. You don't remember that?"

"No. I don't remember you in connection with this at all."

"That's what I thought," Scott said. "You still don't remember things. Lieutenant Hanley, tell me one thing, in your own opinion, do you think you are all right—upstairs?"

Peter took a turn to the door and back again. "That depends on just what you mean, Mr. Scott. The fact is, I don't remember much about what happened. I'm trying to piece it all together."

"The District Attorney isn't going to let you stay here forever. He's really gunning for your hide, you know."

"That's just Tummulty for you. He's out after every conviction he can get. Looks good on the record."

"I'm afraid there's more to it than that," Scott said enigmatically.

"Political ambitions, you mean?"

"No, I'm talking about why he's especially interested in seeing that you get prison—or the chair."

"What has he got against me personally?" Peter was puzzled.

"Maybe he thought you were cutting in on his territory."

"I don't follow you."

"Remember, Lieutenant Hanley, you aren't the only man in town who likes blondes."

"Blondes? You mean Narcissa? You're crazy. She never had anything to do with Dion Tummulty. Where did you ever get a wild idea like that?" Peter took a strong dislike to the way the conversation was heading.

"There might have been some things about Narcissa

Maidstone you just didn't know," Scott said quietly. And then he added, "But we're getting away from what I wanted to speak to you about. I was going to ask you this question: What do you suppose might happen if you had to stand trial?"

"Hmmm?" Peter was preoccupied with other thoughts.

Scott repeated the question.

Peter thought it over for a moment.

"They could convict me—on circumstantial evidence—I guess."

"That's what I feel, too," said Scott. "That would mean a long term in Sing Sing, wouldn't it?" His voice had suddenly softened. "And possibly worse."

"I guess it could."

"It would reflect very badly on the Department. Also on the Commissioner's office."

"Yes?"

"Also be very unpleasant for you."

"What are you getting at?" Peter said with a tinge of anger.

"I've been thinking it might be best for you not to stand trial at all. With the assistance of the doctors here, we might arrange to have you sent away for a while. Long enough for everyone to forget."

"Sent away? Where?"

Scott gave him a long and, Peter thought, a rather fatherly look.

"There are plenty of very comfortable institutions. And in time they might cure you."

Peter stopped, leaned against the maple desk. "Send me to an insane asylum?"

"Well, a kind of rest home," said Scott.

"You can't do that."

"I didn't say we could." Scott's tone was very mild;

the impression he gave was one of benignity, and Peter remembered the stories he had heard of how Scott had often gone to the rescue of police officers in one kind of distress or another. "It was only a suggestion. You might be thinking it over."

He got up, picked up his hat from the dresser, and offered his hand to Peter.

"I think we might have trouble keeping you out of prison," he said. "Except that way."

Peter Hanley said nothing.

"Furthermore," said Scott, "you are not really very well. Do you think so?"

Peter simply stared at him.

"Thanks for your offer, Mr. Scott," he said slowly. "But please go now."

The atmosphere was very heavy and oppressive. After a while he got up and managed to get the shatterproof, suicide-proof windows open an inch or so wider. He could hear the tugboats hooting on the river.

15

Inspector Battle came to see him again. He sat on the same chair as before, put his square hat on his knees, and pulled out his square pipe as before.

"How are things going in the great outside world?" Peter asked with a wry little grin. He was not very self-conscious about the locked doors which surrounded him, or the steel-framed, shatterproof, suicide-proof windows everywhere, but he was a little.

"The same old things," Inspector Battle said. "Nothing ever changes in the Homicide Bureau. I've been in it for thirty-five years and it's just the same as it always was."

"Same old murders."

"Yes, the same old murders. New faces, new names, but the same old cases. Same old motives, too."

Peter grinned. "You're quite a character yourself. Well, tell me what goes on."

Inspector Battle looked out the window, staring as though trying to remember what he had come for. "The D.A. is getting anxious," he said finally.

"Anxious? About what? About me?"

"Yes."

"Well, let him get anxious. Give him some sodium amytal. That does very well for anxiety cases—up to a point. I'm in stir. I'm locked up. I'm under the kind protection of a jury of psychiatrists. They are letting me find out if I killed Narcissa Maidstone. For all the D.A. knows, I'm nuts. For all you know, I'm nuts. For all I know, I'm nuts. George Scott was here several days ago. I guess you know all about it. He says the Commissioner wants me sent to a real first-class Grade A booby hatch."

"Yes, I heard about it. Maybe it isn't too bad an idea."

"Sending me to a nuthouse, you mean?"

"Well," said Inspector Battle, speaking very slowly, "it might be better than Sing Sing."

"Oh, come on now, Inspector! I'd rather go to Sing Sing than a nuthouse any day in the week. You're not giving me up, too, are you?"

"No. I'm just thinking ahead. Figuring out the possibilities.... He's talking about a habeas corpus now."

"Oh. You mean the D.A.?"

"Yes. He wants to get a writ."

"Produce the body, eh? Well, if he's talking about it he'll probably get it. What do you think?"

"That's what I think, too," said Inspector Battle.

"He sure wants to bring me to trial, doesn't he?"

"Very badly."

"Do you know why?" Peter asked, suddenly curious.

"That's beside the point, son. All I know is that he's out after blood. That's why I came here today. I wanted to tell you that time is getting short. I don't want to get you worried but if you can think of anything that might help, now's the time to think of it."

"I guess you're right," Peter said. Then he added, "I haven't been able to think of much so far. It's about as foggy as it ever was. Everything is still all mixed up in my mind."

Then he got to thinking, everything is all mixed up, everything is always all mixed up. And he wondered when, if ever, things would get unmixed, in his mind, his life. Or would the unmixing mean—as the D.A. wanted—his death?

"All we can do is hope for the best then," Inspector Battle was saying.

"Yes, that's right." At least, Inspector Battle was keeping his fingers crossed. "Try to keep the habeas corpus boys away for another four or five days at least," he said.

"I'll try. But why four or five days?"

Peter explained, as well as he could, the mystery of the purple goddess Sodium Amytal, she who presided over dreams, nightmares, delirium, and the hidden memory rooms of the mind that could not be unlocked.

"*In vino veritas*," Peter said. "Or, in other words, booze tells the truth."

"They're not giving you any liquor, are they?" asked Inspector Battle, himself an abstemious man.

"No," said Peter, "but it's the same idea."

"I don't think they ought to give you whisky. You're

bad enough crossed up as it is."

After the Inspector had gone Peter started to walk down the corridor to the East Lounge, but he was intercepted by Miss Dibble. She gave him the mixed look of severity and professional good humor that was characteristic of her.

"We are moving you this evening," she said. "You are to have Professor Tomlinson's corner room. Dr. Holmka wants you to have a little treatment. Beginning Monday."

"Yes, I know," said Peter.

"Would you please get your clothes ready then?"

"Certainly."

He packed all his things and moved them to the room in the southwest corner. It overlooked a rose garden, and beyond the rose garden were the tennis courts of the college. Toward the south and west could be seen the fantastic mass of Rockefeller Center, and farther to the left, the Chrysler Tower.

"This would cost some people plenty," Miss Dibble said. The room was kept strictly for the richer patients.

"It won't cost me plenty," Peter said, "because I haven't got plenty."

After glancing around for a moment, Miss Dibble said, "There'll be an orderly coming up in a few minutes to check your room."

"What's he going to check it for? Little green men?"

Miss Dibble gave him a sour look and went out and he finished packing his shirts away in the dresser drawers and hanging up his suits. The windows were open and there was a cool spicy wind coming in from the southwest. It was the first real touch of autumn.

The orderly was a thin-faced man whom Peter had not seen before around the clinic. But there was something vaguely familiar about him, not only about his build but about his eyes, and Peter was fleetingly reminded of a man he had sent to the chair, very recently sent to the chair. He wore a look of fatuous good humor as though it were a mask, permanently stuck on, to protect himself from all the irritations of his work, his constant contact with whacky or partly whacky people. He had a little kit of tools in his hand.

He gave Peter an empty but good-humored look, and said, "I'm George. I have to check things here."

"That's what Miss Dibble said," Peter remarked, "and I asked her if you were going to look for little green men. I think there are quite a few in here and you ought to get them out."

George did not show that he had got this and, after giving a perfunctory look to the hinges on the door, he went straight to the window.

"Have to check this," he said.

"Why?"

George was humming a little tune and getting out his tools. After a while he said, "Sometimes the bolts get loose."

"And then you can open them wide?"

"Yup."

"And when the bolts get loose the nuts sometimes get loose, too?"

"Yup," the man said, going on with his work. Peter was sorry George had missed the little joke.

George had taken two of the bolts right out and the shatterproof, suicide-proof window swung wide. With the bolts of the cross-irons out, it was wide enough for a man's body.

"I could jump right out there," said Peter.

"Yup," said George. "Come here and look how this works. When it's right, nobody can get out."

Peter crossed the room to the window, saw how the

unbolted irons allowed the window to swing wide. He looked down to the small courtyard below, covered with flagstones and surrounded with shrubbery. If one wished to commit suicide this would be a sure way to do it.

"Aren't you afraid I'll jump?" he said.

"Nope," replied George. Then he added, under his breath, "You ain't going to have the chance."

Peter suddenly found himself pinned against the wall. He felt the strength of apelike arms around him, lifting him up.

"What the hell's the matter with you, you fool?"

But George had no answer, for he was grunting with the exertion of holding Peter's arms and lifting him onto the window sill. Peter, realizing at last that this was no horseplay, began kicking out viciously with his feet, but to no avail. Slowly and inexorably he was being forced across the window sill. After a moment he cried out, but he doubted that there was anyone to hear him. His head was upside down. Buildings swam by his popped-out eyes. Another push would send him hurtling down to the flagstones—to certain death. He no longer dared kick, as kicking would only loosen George's hold.

He heard a voice coming from above him. It was strange-sounding, as though from another world.

"Good coppers are dead coppers."

Then suddenly the hold on his feet was loosened and for a terrible split-second he knew that he was plunging headfirst through the air. Then he knew nothing at all ...

Nothing until he found himself lying on his bed, with Dr. Gatskill standing over him, looking very grave.

"How did all this happen?" she asked.

"George," he said weakly. "George. He's the porter, or the orderly. George did it. Must've gone off his rocker."

"We have no porter named George," said Dr. Gatskill, "nor any orderly by that name."

"No? No orderly named George?" He was still dazed, but the urge was there to protest. "Look, I didn't dream this all up. An orderly named George stuffed me through the window. I *was* shoved out the window, I didn't just imagine it." There was no doubt in his mind on that score. His body ached all over.

"Yes, you did fall from the window."

"And it was a long way down." Once more the courtyard swam before his eyes. He closed them tightly, trying to shut out the vision. He shuddered as he relived the moment of his fall.

"What is it?" Dr. Gatskill asked tensely.

"Nothing," Peter said, coming out of it. "Except that by all rights I ought to be dead, hadn't I?"

"Definitely," Dr. Gatskill said. "And if you hadn't fallen close to the wall and caught in the limbs of a plane tree you would have been, too. As it was, you were knocked cold and it took a long time to get you out of the tree."

"What happened to George?"

"That's another story," said Dr. Gatskill. "George doesn't belong to us. He doesn't belong to the hospital. He's somebody who belongs to you. Do you have any idea who George is?"

"No." But he remembered abruptly the resemblance George bore to a man he'd sent to the electric chair, a man named Shorty Cerwin, and he recollected other times when the relative of a convicted killer had tried to even up scores.

"Do you have any idea who might have sent him?"

"No." No sense saying anything to her; to anybody. George wouldn't come back. Would there be somebody else? And he began feeling himself all over, and found that he was bruised in nearly every spot he touched.

Dr. Gatskill stood silent for a moment, gazing down at him. Then she said, "You can solve all this yourself. The solution is in your mind."

"That's what you've told me. Why don't I solve it then?"

Her gaze softened and the violet eyes seemed to become warm and sympathetic. "We're trying, Lieutenant Hanley. We're trying very hard."

And then she went out with the swish of starch and the twinkle of blue shoes.

16

On Monday morning he was not given any breakfast. Instead, the laboratory girl, Miss Simmons, came and, pricking his finger, took a bright-red ruby drop of blood and smeared it on a panel of glass.

Then there was the rabbit test. This was not taken by the technician but by a staff doctor, a woman doctor named Dr. Bundschu. She tied a bit of rubber tubing around his arm and took out a syringe with a wicked needle. She began searching about for a vein.

"This is what they call the rabbit test, isn't it?" Peter said, to make conversation. "Supposed to show one's anxiety, or something like that."

"Yes, something like that." She took the needle out, gave him a blob of cotton to hold on the tiny wound. Then she peered at a rash on his forearm. "You have an eczema."

"Yes," he replied. "I got a bullet through my arm one

time. Once in a while it comes up in a rash."

Dr. Bundschu began putting her materials in order.

"I, too," she said, "was shot in the arm once. A patient did it. In Vienna. But I never have any eczema. Do you suppose your eczema could come from the way you think?"

"No, I don't," Peter said, exasperated. "The bullet wound interfered with the circulation and that's why I get the rash. At least," he added, "that's what a real doctor told me once."

"Well," she said, putting his blood into a bottle, "I suppose that's possible, medically speaking. But anxiety causes a great deal of eczema, too. Didn't you know that?"

And, with her curious smile, she went out the door. He sat thinking about what she had said, and especially that preposterous statement about having been shot by a patient. That was simply too much.

He had been instructed not to dress. So he sat on the edge of his bed and smoked cigarettes until Miss Dibble appeared with his breakfast.

"For the doomed man?" he asked.

Miss Dibble did not see any humor in this. "You are not to get dressed this morning," she said.

"Yes. You told me that once."

She put the tray on his maple writing desk. "Dr. Holmka will be here at ten. Right after the staff conference."

"Oh. That's nice. That's very nice. The full treatment, eh?"

"What do you mean?"

"The chief. I get the chief."

"I expect your own doctor will be in on it too," she said.

"Dr. Gatskill?"

"Yes. Maybe some other doctors, too."

"Oh. Is it that important?"

"No. It isn't very." Miss Dibble was an eager deflator of egos; always on guard, ready to pounce, if anyone so much as hinted they wanted personal attention. Peter sometimes wondered about this. Everyone needed at least a little attention to exist as human beings, didn't they? What was Miss Dibble's motive in trying to deny it? Was she acting as an agent of the psychological machinery of this clinic or only as an agent of Miss Dibble's own ego?

After a while she came back, took away the breakfast tray, and later returned with a hypodermic and a box marked *Sodium Amytal*. She took an ampule out of the box and began fixing up a potion.

"Well, I guess you'll be having fun," she said.

"Will I?"

"It's like being on a two-day binge. Some people beg for it."

"Do they? Who? What people?"

She pursed her lips. No comments were ever made here about other patients. She asked him to relax his arm and then gave him the shot.

"Now you just lie still," she said. "And whatever you do, don't try going into the hall. You might fall and hurt yourself. Dr. Holmka will be in to see you in a few minutes. Meanwhile, just relax."

"All right." His tongue already felt rather thick.

Miss Dibble went out, closing the door behind her. It was a thick door and it shut out all the noises of the corridor. It also kept passers-by from listening in on the "psychotherapy"—a very important item, too, since few people would feel much like turning their little ids inside out if they thought there were eavesdroppers.

Peter lay back and relaxed. This was not hard to do, as the insidious drug began to operate, making a slow sleepy smoldering fire in his blood. The barbiturates, he had been told, operate on the central nervous system, and they also had the effect of cutting out the inhibitory centers of the mind—the reasoning faculties—thus allowing the true emotions to come to the surface. Alcohol did the same thing, but it was harder to control and also the individual's reaction was more erratic.

His legs and arms began to feel heavy, and his eyes were drowsy. Little dream-images began floating across his mind; they were elusive and fascinating. He wondered if he ought to fight off this wonderful drowsiness, but he decided he couldn't if he wanted to.

The clouds had gathered again, and the rain had begun. It was coming down with a swishing sound that blotted out all the traffic sounds. The room was quite dark. The rain began making a droning sound in his ears.

He was in a long car, built like an ambulance, and he was lying down looking at a motion picture screen. He could feel the motion of the car as it went up and down hills and around bends. Dr. Holmka seemed to be sitting beside him, only it was not really Dr. Holmka, but only a little flicker of light. It was Dr. Holmka's personality, but it was really just a little flicker of light.

"I want to show you something," said the flicker of light, using no words but somehow communicating with him. "Look at the screen, please."

There was a roar, and flames seemed to rise on the motion picture screen. At the same time the car began pitching violently, and Peter clung tightly to the rails beside him. The sensation of imminent doom was terrific, the whole world was running away with him, and he whispered, "Stop it! Stop it!" But the car went plunging up and down, the flames seemed to be leaping out of the screen.

Then suddenly it all stopped and he felt that the flickering little light was smiling faintly.

"Now we shall see what we shall see," it said. "Don't hide your eyes. God is everywhere, God is both beautiful and ugly, God is everything. Now look at the screen, please."

The car was gliding gently now and Peter had the sensation of going through sun-bathed valleys.

He looked at the screen. At first it was pure white, but then there arose a single word in letters of fire. It started very small but it came up quickly to huge proportions, and filled not only the screen but the whole room. The word was *Fear*, and the presence of this flaming word was overwhelming.

He sank back on the pillow and the car was gliding gently through the sun-bathed countryside. The little flickering light beside him was smiling faintly. Peter closed his eyes, and then he could hear the rain swishing down. He opened his eyes again and saw that he was in his room. He had been dreaming but he was not sure, at the moment, just how much of it had been a dream, for he saw that Dr. Holmka was indeed beside him. The gold pen was in his hand.

"Did you say something?" Peter asked. "What did you say?"

"I didn't say anything," said Dr. Holmka in his quiet Viennese way. "But you did. You said the word *fear*."

"Did I?" Peter asked. "Well, I was dreaming about it, I guess."

"Do you think about fear a great deal?" Dr. Holmka asked.

"No. Of course not." His voice was thick and strange-sounding.

"Do you think fear has anything to do with your present trouble?"

"I don't know. Could be. I don't know exactly how."

"Fear is at the bottom of a good many things," said Dr. Holmka, turning his pen around. Peter watched its gold glint in the dark room.

"I suppose it is," Peter said. "But I don't feel afraid of anything."

"Were you afraid of anything in your childhood?"

"No. Nothing that I can think of. My mother sometimes. And Father Lanihan."

"Father who?"

"Father Lanihan. He was the parish priest at St. Joseph's. But you couldn't call it being afraid."

"You might, if you examine it."

Peter was silent, and he examined it. "No, I don't think so."

"Were you afraid of Narcissa Maidstone?" Dr. Holmka's voice was like the flickering light in the car. It was insistent, intense, vibrant—but very soft and gentle. "Were you afraid of Narcissa Maidstone?"

"Afraid of her?" He heard his own voice, thick and distant. "I don't know how I could have been afraid of her. Unless it was in some obscure way that I don't understand."

"What do you mean by that?"

"I don't know."

"You said it. You must know what you meant."

"But I don't. I wish I hadn't said it."

The doctor said nothing. Peter's eyes were half shut. He was very drowsy. What was that question? What was he afraid of? Narcissa Maidstone? His mother? Father Lanihan?

The rain drummed against the window and swished down through the leaves. Down, down the rain, come down the rain. And through the rain, pinwheels, whirling at him in the darkness ... spinning ... whirling ...

Father Lanihan met him on the church steps. There were a whole lot of other little boys and little girls, too, but Father Lanihan spoke only to him. It was his first communion.

Father Lanihan took his hand. "This is a great day for you, Peter." It was a hearty Sunday morning voice, quite different from the soft intimate whisper of the confessional the evening before.

Peter did not reply. He was seven and a half years old and he was frightened by the awful majesty he was about to meet. God came down and spoke to you at the altar rail. *Corpus domine ... Corpus domine* mumble mumble mutter mutter. *Corpus domine*.

There was a choir and it sang "O Lord I am not worthy," and down to the altar rail they went two by two, the little boys and the little girls; and after it was all over he walked home, the feeling of the wafer lingering in his mouth, and for a while he felt that he was vastly changed. He no longer was the careless little boy that he had been, and his heart swelled with new dignity. But at the corner of Water Street there were some kids playing stick ball, and he forgot about the sensation of the wafer, and the new dignity, too. He began to play with the boys. Soon he fell down and tore the knee in his white pants and when he got home his mother whipped him with the razor strop.

Of all the kids in the parish, Father Lanihan had

taken a liking to him, little Peter Hanley. And Peter liked Father Lanihan, too. Next to his mother and Sergeant Quinlan he guessed Father Lanihan was the one he liked best.

He was twelve or thirteen, and it was not a Sunday but a weekday, and as he was passing by the church Father Lanihan stopped him.

"Where are you going, Peter?" he asked.

"Just going to the store for Ma, Father."

"Come here and sit on the steps for a minute, Peter."

He dutifully did as he was asked. It was a hot New York day, but not muggy; the sky was clear and all the sounds were sharp. They could hear the river sounds, and the market sounds, and the clatter of the "el," and there was a faint smell of brine from the waterfront. They sat in the great black shadow of the church and looked across the street where the sun glared on Addonizio's pharmacy, and Dimassi's pizza pie café, and on Ching Lo's hand laundry. A Good Humor man had parked his little white ice-cream cart next to the curb and two little girls were walking round and round it, trying to make up their minds as to just what they wanted.

"I have been thinking about you, Peter," said Father Lanihan.

Peter did not reply.

"I have been thinking maybe you would like being an altar boy. Would you like that, Peter?"

"I guess so."

Father Lanihan put his plump hand on Peter's knee. He was a round man who wore thick eyeglasses, and they gave him a peering, inquisitive, but kindly look. He was not at all like Father Murtagh, who was dour and harsh, or like Father Cocchia, who had big pools of watery eyes and skin like a wax candle, and who generally smelled of garlic.

"Have you ever thought about what you might be when you grow up?" Father Lanihan asked.

Peter had already decided he was going to be a policeman, but he said, "No, Father, I ain't."

"You mean haven't," Father Lanihan said, folding his chubby hands. "*Haven't* is the correct word. Do you think you might ever study for the priesthood?"

"No, I never thought of that."

"The priesthood needs good men," Father Lanihan said, and then added, artfully, "And I think you are a good man."

Peter felt a little lump of pride in his throat. It was not the idea of the priesthood so much that pleased him; it was those words: "I think you are a good man."

He cleared his throat and his treble voice broke.

"Your voice is changing," Father Lanihan observed mildly. "Next thing you know, you'll be shaving. Well, what about it?"

"I ain't never talked it over with Ma," Peter said. "What I'm going to be, I mean."

"The word is *haven't*," said Father Lanihan. "Well, I wish you would start thinking about it. Remember— a priest gives up a great deal, but he gains a great deal, too."

"Yes, I guess that's right."

They both stood up.

"You think it over, my boy," Father Lanihan said.

"All right, Father, I will."

And he went off toward home, picturing himself wearing a cassock like Father Lanihan, or wearing the vestments of the Mass.

But nothing ever came of it. He was an altar boy for a while, but he really could not face the thought of becoming a priest.

"I was afraid," he said to himself. "I was afraid of something."

The little light beside him flickered and seemed to incline toward him, as though bent by a slight breeze.

"What were you afraid of? You said you were afraid." The question was whispered but intense. "What were you afraid of?"

"I don't know. I guess I was just afraid of being a priest."

"Didn't want to live a life of celibacy? Was that it?"

There was a silence—then he heard his voice coming thick and far away.

"No. I don't think it was that. I really don't think it was that."

"What were you afraid of, then?"

"I guess—I guess I was afraid I wasn't good enough."

"Not capable enough—or not good enough, morally?"

It was a long time before his voice came. Then it was very small and distant. He thought it was one of the raindrops speaking.

"Morally," the raindrop said.

Then there was just the swishing and splatter at the windows.

"I see," Dr. Holmka said.

17

Julius Hassenpepper had an apartment on Park Avenue and it cost a pile of money to maintain. Where Julius Hassenpepper got the pile of money was nobody's business; or rather, everybody's business.

When Peter Hanley reached the apartment, Julius Hassenpepper was in a position never to have to worry about the rent again. Or the light bill, or which picture hung where on the wall. He was, in fact, in the ideal position never to have to worry about anything at all. He was dead.

The body of this evil little man, whose power extended into City Hall, into the Police Department, and even into the Congress of the United States as well as across two continents in a filthy network of crime and vice and corruption, lay flat on its face on the floor. The little emperor of evil was dead, and lying there on his expensive carpet he looked as undignified as a sack of potatoes.

"Death be not proud," muttered Peter.

"What did you say?" asked Sergeant O'Keefe, as stupid a man as was ever born.

"I didn't say it, John Donne said it."

"Dunn ain't here," said O'Keefe. "He ain't even on the case."

Peter watched the cameraman from the Identification Bureau fussing around with his camera, and then he began to prowl around the room.

This man whom he now met in death he had once met in life—and later wished that it had never happened.

In those days Peter was younger. More eager and more rash. He had, as a very junior person in the Department, contemplated the workings of the Hassenpepper empire from afar, had seen its terrible evil and its awful power, and had wished that he could do something to break it.

There was a murder—quite a routine affair, really—and it was one of Peter's earliest cases. A young man by the name of Hacko Judson was fished out of the East River one morning shortly before the sun came up. The odd thing about the Hacko Judson case was that he was ever fished up at all, for, besides having been stabbed twenty-one times with a long knife, his head being bashed in, and having been shot twice through the temples, he had been wired up, encased in concrete, and further weighted with short lengths of railroad ties.

It was upon this occasion that Chips Galligan of *The Daily Mail* had made his classic remark. Staring at Hacko Judson on the wharf at the foot of James Slip, Chips Galligan said, "Looks like foul play."

Mr. Hacko Judson, in the condition which had inspired this comment, had interfered with the anchor chains of the *S.S. Auvergne*, whose skipper had reported the whole annoying matter in a kind of bastard but highly effective brand of English he had picked up in his youth on the wharves of Marseilles.

It was not a very interesting case, except for the thoroughgoing manner of it, until Peter ran into a character known as Two Bit MacNeish in Smokey's Bar and Tavern, near the Fulton Street Market which, wholly by coincidence, was near the scene of the discovery of the body.

Two Bit MacNeish led Peter out of the bar and along South Street and, not wishing it to appear that he was in conversation with a copper, further led him up a blind alleyway.

"Hacko was my pal," said Two Bit, "or I wouldn't be telling you nothin'. He was workin' for a gent named Julius Hassenpepper. Hassenpepper hired Hacko to knock off a wrongie truck driver named Budd. Billy the Kid Budd. To make a long story short, Hacko didn't knock off Billy—and so Hassenpepper sent out the word. That's why you found Hacko sitting in a concrete box at the bottom of the river."

There was more of the same, with considerable

circumstantial detail. Peter thanked Two Bit and bought him, by way of a five-dollar bill which he could ill spare, enough drinks to compensate for the loss of his time. Peter began to work the case over in his own mind, to see where it led.

He knew where it led, and after a week's checking up it still led in the same direction—to Julius Hassenpepper.

Julius Hassenpepper's power placed him, in a way, above and beyond the law, by means which unhappily have become familiar in American cities: he let officialdom into the proceeds of his enormous enterprises, and at the same time cloaked himself in an air of infinite propriety. Nobody but a very young detective would have thought of going to see Julius Hassenpepper about a cheap little murder like that of Hacko Judson. That was no doubt why he got into the apartment so easily.

"I'm Lieutenant Hanley," he said.

Julius Hassenpepper was smoking a long thin cigar and he gave Peter a weary look and said in a thin whining voice, "Please to meet you, Lieutenant. But I don't wish to take any more tickets to the Policemen's Ball. And already I sent a check for the Police Athletic League. Enough is enough."

"That isn't what I want to talk to you about," said Peter. "I want to talk about the murder of a fellow named Hacko Judson."

"Murder?" said Julius. "How could I know anything about a murder?"

Peter's attitude became a trifle hostile. "I have information," he said, "that you know a lot about this particular murder. And I came to find out—"

"Please, please, Lieutenant!" Hassenpepper exclaimed. "I am not deaf." He pronounced it "deef."

Then he picked up the phone, dialed a number, waited. "Commissioner?" he said. "Oh, Mr. Scott! No, I don't mind talking to you. George, this is Julius. I'm fine, George. But, George, there's a young lieutenant here by the name of Hanley, wishes to question me about something. About a murder, he said. Now, I don't— Yes, yes, George, I'll put him on."

George Scott's voice was thin and unpleasant. "This is the Commissioner's office," he said. "Who gave you your orders on this?"

"Nobody, but—"

"I advise you to report back to your superior officers at once."

The phone clicked. Peter Hanley, angry and humiliated, left the Hassenpepper apartment without another word. Several days later he received for all his pains a departmental reprimand, in writing.

And now here he was with Julius Hassenpepper again. It was no longer possible for Julius to phone the Commissioner's office.

The cause of his death was quite simple. It was a bullet through that evil little brain.

"Looks like a .32-caliber bullet," Peter said. "What do you think?"

Sergeant O'Keefe nodded. "You're right as rain. A .32-caliber bullet done it."

"Have you found the slug?"

"What? Oh, the slug. No, but I guess it ain't far."

Peter studied the corpse from several angles. Then he said, "No, not far."

O'Keefe peered at him. "Well, where do you think it is?"

"It's still in the brain. It never came out anywhere."

"Jeez," said O'Keefe. "Pretty smart guy, ain't you? What makes you think it never came out anywhere?"

"That's simple enough—one hole. If it had come out there would be two holes in the head."

When the autopsy was eventually performed, that was exactly where the .32-caliber slug was found—in the center of Julius Hassenpepper's brain.

At the apartment, Peter Hanley set to work. Someone—obviously no genius himself—has said that genius consists of an infinite capacity for hard work, and the same is true when it comes to solving a crime. It is not done with mirrors or black magic or Sherlock Holmes deductions, but by the accumulation, the examination, and the evaluation of masses of detail.

There was one rather large detail in the Julius Hassenpepper apartment at the time of the crime. She was a big blond woman named Griselda Cunningham, and where she fitted into the picture was not quite clear, but Peter Hanley proposed to find out.

"Where is she?" he asked.

Sergeant O'Keefe's lips curled slightly. "Suppose you think we let her skip."

"I didn't think," said Peter. "I just asked."

"Well, she's in the other room, playing hearts with Oleson."

"Hearts, eh? Nice game. Appropriate, too. Well, I guess I'd better talk to her."

He went in and Oleson went out.

It was a wide room which looked like a library or a study. The woman sat on a sofa smoking a cigarette, and before her on a low coffee table there was a scatter of cards. She was big and blond and she had shiny hazel eyes like a cat's.

"I'm Lieutenant Hanley of the Homicide Bureau. Who are you?"

"Is that a polite question?" she asked. "After all, this

is my apartment."

"Is it? That's an interesting point. But I didn't come to ask polite questions." He sat down opposite her, stared most impolitely. "What's your name and where do you fit into the picture?"

She gave him a long look from beneath heavy and slightly puffy eyelids. "I don't know anything," she said shortly.

"You'll have to talk so you may as well tell me. I listen good. I suppose you know your name."

"Griselda Cunningham."

"That's an odd name," Peter said. "What are you? What's your background?"

Her eyes glinted. She put out her cigarette in a large square ash tray of Swedish glass. Her fingers were long but not artistic or sensitive; on the contrary, they gave the impression of great strength. She should have been a lady wrestler with those fingers, Peter thought.

"Is all this necessary—and official?" she asked.

"Yes, it's necessary—and murder makes it official." Peter took out a sack of Bull Durham and a package of papers. He rolled a cigarette slowly, then twisted the end.

Her eyes showed a glitter of amusement. "Hopalong Cassidy?" she said. "Or Tom Mix?"

"You remember as far back as Tom Mix?"

Her lips set again in a thin line and the little trace of humor went out of her eyes. "I remember a lot of things. What are you going to ask me?"

Peter lighted his cigarette. "When I first spoke to you, you told me this was your home or something like that."

"That's right."

"Just what is your position in this household, Miss

Cunningham?"

"Come again?"

"What is your relationship to Julius Hassenpepper?"

"Oh," she said, "I'm kind of a housekeeper, I guess. Kind of a glorified housekeeper."

"Glorified? What does that mean?"

She sat back on the sofa, giving him another long look. Then she took out another cigarette, lighted it, and blew smoke through her rather wide, flaring nostrils.

"All right, I guess I have to talk sooner or later. You asked me what I was to Julius and I told you. Glorified housekeeper. That's what it wound up amounting to."

"Wound up?"

"You wanted me to talk, didn't you? I'm talking."

"All right. Talk."

"A long time ago I meant something to him. That's when he didn't have much money—and he needed me. We lived in a little apartment on Third Avenue, over a delicatessen, right near Fifty-eighth Street. He wanted to marry me. Can you imagine that? Julius Hassenpepper wanted to marry me."

Peter gave her a keen look. "Yes? Well, why didn't you marry him? What was the gimmick?"

"I was afraid."

"Afraid of what?"

Her eyes shifted toward the other room. There was an odd, unpleasant glitter in them. "Afraid of something like what finally happened."

"I don't get it," Peter said. "It doesn't sound reasonable that you would be stopped from marrying him from such a farfetched fear as that."

"Farfetched!" Her deep voice suddenly became shrill. "Look, Lieutenant, I don't look stupid, do I?"

"No. Definitely not."

"Well, listen then. That was a long time ago but I saw the road Julius was traveling. He was in the small time then but he was on the road. The same road that ended there in that room, on the floor. In those days he was financing a couple of horse books, had his finger in a two-bit dope deal and one thing and another. He didn't tell me anything—but I could use my eyes and my head. I could see where he was heading."

There was a distant look in her hazel eyes as she went on: "I didn't want to get tangled up with him. I didn't want to be married to a guy who looked to me like a living dead man. I figured he'd end up on a rubbish dump or in the river or somewhere, and I didn't want to be really tied to him. I told myself I'd stick around a while and then some day I'd blow. But I never could. I might as well have been married to him. The fact is, I couldn't live without him."

"You loved him?"

"I guess that's the word for it." She made a funny little gesture with her hands. It was a fluttering kind of gesture and it was funny because she was not a fluttering kind of person. "Well, you see how it turned out."

"Yes, I see how it turned out, all right."

"So," she said, lighting another cigarette, "you asked me to tell you something and I told you something. Everything, in fact."

"Well, not quite everything. For instance, where were you when all this happened?"

"I was in the bedroom. In my own bedroom."

"Tell me about it."

She spoke in a monotone, sleepily, smoking cigarette after cigarette. Her puffy eyelids, with a touch of blue on them, were often half shut as she told him about it.

Julius Hassenpepper had reached a lofty summit in his drive for power. He was a little man physically and a little man in many other ways, too, but he had a shrewdness composed of a very big thing inside him: a thing called avarice. As an immigrant boy he had known the bitterest privations, and it was the intense fear of poverty at the very core of his heart that had driven him to become the man that he was.

His first enterprise, at the age of eighteen, was making book on the horses, and as headquarters he hung around a place called Uncle Ed's, on Second Avenue just above Eightieth. This was during Prohibition, and Uncle Ed's was ostensibly a cigar store and soft drink counter which actually sold, to an elite clientele, moonshine whisky, homemade gin, and a vicious concoction known as grappa.

Julius had no scruples, and by scraping and manipulating he soon got himself out of the direct business into that of financing those who make book. It was but a step from this to financing liquor smugglers and speakeasy operators and, when Prohibition ended, it was but a small step back to financing gamblers. By that time his wealth was great, and also his power. He invested a little money here and there in legitimate business, and adopted a cloak of rectitude inviolate.

Thus Julius Hassenpepper rose from the gutters of the upper East Side to the gutters of Park Avenue.

Peter thought about all that, and about the case of Hacko Judson, and how quickly Hassenpepper had got action from the office of the commissioner of police.

Well, here was the man now, flat on his face, with a .32-caliber bullet in the middle of his head.

Peter turned back to consider Griselda Cunningham. "You were in the bedroom. Just what happened?"

Griselda gave him her hard and glittering stare. "I really don't know. If I did I would tell you."

"Well, tell me as far as you know."

"All right. It was around three o'clock in the morning when Julius came home. There's nothing unusual in that. He generally gets in about that hour. This time there were a couple of people with him."

"Is that unusual?"

"No, it's not. He spends—he spent—his evenings around the night spots and he was always bringing someone home with him."

"What kind of people?"

"Oh. Just anybody. I seldom saw them."

"This night? Did you see them?"

"No."

"Well, what happened?"

"I was lying in bed reading—waiting for things to quiet down. I heard Julius go to the kitchen for ice and drinks. There were two people—a man and a girl. They were talking in low tones."

"Did you hear what they said?"

"No."

"Why did you use the expression *girl* instead of *woman?* What made you think it was a girl?"

"Oh. I can tell. I'm allergic to other women around the place. And girls."

"Jealous?"

She bit her lip. "Yes," she said. "I don't—didn't—mean anything to Julius, not anymore, but I was jealous just the same."

"I see. What happened next?"

"I heard Julius take in the drinks. There was a little talk. Then I thought I heard a funny sound—like the popping of a paper bag when you blow it up with air. But not much of a sound, really. I didn't pay any attention to it then. I could hear the man and the girl talking and then they went out. I didn't hear Julius, and I began thinking it was funny I hadn't heard him say good night or anything to the couple."

"What did you do?"

"I listened for a long time. Just listened. I began to get scared. We have two maids but they don't sleep in. So there was just me in the apartment—just me and Julius."

"What did you do then?"

"I got up, put on my robe. I went into the living room—and found Julius just as you saw him."

Peter looked at her keenly. "Then you called the cops. Is that right?"

"Yes. That's right." She sat staring at her feet for a moment. "That's all. That's all there is. There isn't any more. Look, copper. Are you putting me under arrest?"

Peter Hanley studied her for quite a while. Then he said, "No. I'm not. Not yet anyhow. But you will have to report to us regularly—or we'll pick you up as a material witness. Don't leave town."

"Why not?"

"Just don't do it. We'll make you wish you hadn't. Okay?"

"Okay."

He left her then. He spoke briefly with Sergeant O'Keefe and Oleson, and looked at Julius Hassenpepper, who was still posing for the birdie and waiting, patiently enough, for the medical examiner. Emperor of Evil, Lord of Vice and Corruption, flat on his face and dead as a mackerel.

At the Homicide Bureau he walked in on Inspector Battle, who was holding the phone.

"This is for you," he said.

A voice like sandpaper said, "This Lieutenant Peter

Hanley?"

"Yes."

"Look here, Lieutenant Peter Hanley, I got something to say to you."

"All right. Say it."

"You remember Hacko Judson?"

"Yes."

"Well, you keep your hands off the Hassenpepper deal or you'll look just like Hacko Judson. Only more concrete and farther down the river. Get it? More concrete and farther down the river."

The receiver clicked. Inspector Battle had tried to trace the call, but it turned out to be a phone booth in the old Times Building at Forty-Second and Broadway. When the radio car got there, there was nothing in the booth but the smell of cigar smoke.

Peter looked at Inspector Battle and said, "They must think I scare easy. Maybe I do, but not that easy."

A slow crinkly grin spread over Inspector Battle's face.

18

The room was dark. Quite dark. There was no rain now. Only the skittering of the wind at the curtains. Far off, like elfin horns, were the muffled hoots of the taxis and cars. Peter Hanley was incapable of thought, and yet he thought—or felt—that it was evening.

There were violet eyes, and mingled with the distant hooting of the taxis there was a small bell-like voice.

"That frightened you, didn't it? You were afraid then, weren't you?"

"I'm not frightened. I'm not afraid. Why should I be?"

"What you said was, 'I don't scare easy.' Would that mean you were really afraid?"

"Afraid? No. What could I be afraid of?"

"I don't know. Were you afraid of looking like Hacko Judson? Stabbed, shot, wired up in concrete, and lying on the bottom of the East River?"

Peter raised his head off the pillow, sat up in bed. He began weaving a little, so he held on to the bedrails, peering out in the gloom at her.

"Who told you about that?"

"You did. You just told me."

"Oh."

He sank back on the pillow. He felt dreadful. There was a horrible taste in his mouth and he realized that he wanted another shot of that dope. He saw how people could get the habit. He was having a sodium amytal hangover, and it was the worst kind he had ever had.

He said, "You think I'm afraid of something, don't you?"

"Do you think you are?"

"No. I don't."

"Well, then—" She switched on the little light beside the table, and he put his hands over his eyes. "We will give you a little supper now. Are you feeling uncomfortable?"

"Very."

"Well, we will make you more comfortable."

"Thanks. Thanks a lot." She started to go, but he lifted his head again and called her. There was something he wanted desperately to know.

"Doctor, are you finding out anything?"

Dr. Gatskill paused with her hand on the doorknob. "Are you? Are you finding out anything, Mr. Hanley?"

The door closed gently behind her, and he was alone

with the little blob of yellow light on the bedside table and the skittering of the wind at the curtains.

Miss Lupino, the night nurse, came with a trayful of supper. It was very dainty and yet he could bring himself to eat only a little of it. Then Miss Lupino began preparing the familiar hypodermic. After she slid the needle in he lay back and waited for the wonderful, comfortable drunken drowsiness. The light was still on but it no longer bothered him. He listened to the skittering of the wind and after a while he thought Dr. Holmka was beside him. He was not sure. It was just a little flame, like the flame of a candle, bent toward him by the wind.

He was standing on Australia, and flames had spread over the earth, over all the continents and islands of the earth, seven times, and there was the dreadful possibility that they would sweep around once again. Standing on Australia, he read about it all in the headlines, and then he saw that the occasion was indeed desperate, for God and Mrs. God had set up a tower high above the earth, to show themselves to the frightened people. Peter looked at the tower and God gave him a dirty baleful look and then Peter realized that he had caused it all. He, Peter Hanley, had caused it all because there was a deep kind of poison in his soul which had spread and caused the ruin of the world.

He had to travel to all the burned-over continents, to accept the blame and the guilt for it all.

He looked toward the tower where God high above the earth was directing the rescue and the salvage and reassuring the people. But now God was a little candlelight wavering in the wind and inclining toward him.

"Is that what you were afraid of?"

He did not hear what Dr. Holmka was saying. He had already set out to go to all the continents and accept the blame. Everywhere the earth was hot from the seven fires.

He did not suffer the fate of Hacko Judson, did not get a knife in his back, a bullet in his heart, or go to the bottom of the East River encased in concrete.

But in the solution, if it could be called a solution, and officially it was, of the death of Julius Hassenpepper he got no great amount of help from any quarter, and especially none from any of those persons who had been Julius Hassenpepper's friends in life. The only help he got was from his own stubborn determination.

In the end it was little Shorty Cerwin, a small and evil man of no consequence, who burned at Sing Sing for the murder, and though the Hassenpepper case was officially closed, still there were grave and unofficial doubts in Peter Hanley's mind.

Oh, Shorty Cerwin was guilty, there was no doubt about that. It was his .32-caliber Mauser, and there was the strongest possible chain of circumstantial evidence to show that he fired the shot. But who else was guilty? Not Shorty Cerwin alone. And what of the girl whose voice Griselda Cunningham had heard in the room that night with Julius Hassenpepper? The girl with the voice never came into the picture at all.

In the Homicide Bureau under the hard lights, without food and water, Shorty Cerwin at last said that he did it, because even his crooked little mind could not twist out of the straitjacket of bitter logic which Peter Hanley's case had put it in. But he denied there was anyone else, anybody who hired him, anybody who accompanied him, anybody at all. In the Homicide Bureau under the pitiless lights he denied it, and in the witness chair, under the cruel and clever probing of the then Assistant District Attorney, Dion Tummulty, he still denied it.

But the others nevertheless existed. There was a man who did the hiring, who bought a passage for Julius Hassenpepper into the next world, and there was a girl. She existed too. How did he know?

It was all there, implicit in the case, but it could not be traced to its conclusion, could not be proved, so Shorty Cerwin burned alone at Sing Sing, and the Julius Hassenpepper murder was officially entered as closed.

He saw Inspector Battle grinning at him.

"You've got a woman on the brain."

"Yes. I have," he admitted, and sat down beside the inspector. This was at the beginning of the case, before Shorty Cerwin had been arrested, before his trail had even been scented.

"Why are you so sure about this woman?" asked Inspector Battle. "Why are you sure Griselda Cunningham wasn't talking through her hat?"

"She could've been," Peter replied. "But I don't think so. And there are two things that make me not think so."

"Yes? Well—like what?"

"For one, the elevator operator. He saw two people go up with Julius the night he was killed."

"Yes, I know that. That's in the report."

"Then there's something else in the report. But nobody has paid any attention to it."

"What's that?"

"Well, there was a little gadget found in that

apartment. It was just a little thing that most women carry, and I guess that's why you and the rest of the gang around here didn't pay attention to it."

"All right, all right," said Inspector Battle, "what was it?"

"I've got it here. I took it out of the evidence safe."

"You're not supposed to do that."

"If I never did anything but what I was supposed to do I'd never get anything done," said Peter. "Look."

He took a small object out of his pocket. It gleamed with a golden glint.

Inspector Battle took it into his hand, turning it over several times in his methodical manner.

"A lipstick holder," he said. "What use is that to us? They're a dime a dozen—and all alike. They produce these things by the thousands. One wouldn't mean anything to us. Could belong to anybody."

"Look again," said Peter. "This one wasn't mass-produced and it didn't belong to just anyone. There's probably only one of its kind. Look at it."

Inspector Battle's face began to light up slowly. "It's gold, isn't it? Real fourteen-carat gold."

"It's gold, all right."

"And it has a—what do you call it—a cameo on the side."

"No. That's not a cameo," said Peter. "It's an intaglio."

"What's the difference?"

"An intaglio is just the opposite of a cameo. In a cameo, the figure or design is in relief, it's raised. In an intaglio it's cut into the stone, or the material. In this case it's etched."

"You're pretty smart," the inspector said. "How did you find out all this?"

"I did a little checking."

"Find the manufacturer?"

"No. Not yet. There's no manufacturer's name on it. But I talked to some jewelers about it. This thing is solid gold, the work is all original handwork, and it was probably quite expensive. It was made to order, most likely by a craftsman in a small shop, and there was probably a companion piece—a gold compact with the same intaglio design on it."

"That what the jewelers told you?"

"Yes. They can't be sure there was a companion piece. But they think it unlikely that it would be made any other way."

Inspector Battle leaned back in his chair, studying the intaglio lipstick holder. "Then the thing to do is try to find out who made it."

"Yes, and the next step after that is to find the companion piece, the intaglio compact."

"It would be nice if we could do that," Inspector Battle said as he studied the carving of a woman's head, cut in a little black curved plaque, affixed to the gold. "By the way, who is this supposed to be?"

"Diana," replied Peter. "Goddess of the Hunt."

"Oh."

They both lapsed into silence hypnotized by the small gleaming object in Inspector Battle's hands. The blue tobacco smoke made a kind of wreath around it.

19

There was no real obvious reason why Griselda Cunningham could not have killed Julius Hassenpepper. And yet Peter Hanley was convinced that she did not, had not, could not, was wholly incapable of it. This matter of being incapable— psychologically incapable—was one of the intangibles of his business, and yet it was a matter which every police officer takes into account, consciously or otherwise, in the examination of a crime. It can fool you, it can blow up in your face, but in the contemplation of every suspect in relation to the crime a police officer must inevitably ask himself, "Could this person have done this? Could this *kind* of a person do this *kind* of a thing?"

Peter Hanley asked himself this question about Griselda, and while he saw that in the mere physical circumstances of the case she was the most logical person, the one in the best position to have killed Julius Hassenpepper, yet he did not believe her capable of it. She was the woman who merely stuck around. Chances were strongly against her having killed Julius Hassenpepper.

Time and events might have proved him wrong on this point, but they did not. Time and events led into something more complicated and more sinister than the personal motives of a cast-off sweetheart.

"Was there something about the intaglio box you were afraid of?"

Peter saw the little flicker of light incline toward him and he sat up in bed holding on to the bed rail because he was so groggy. He was also very angry.

"You keep asking that stupid question! Why should there be anything about the intaglio box that I should be afraid of? What made you think that?"

Dr. Holmka's voice came very quietly: "I didn't think anything at all. I just asked a question. Well, tell me, did the intaglio box lead you anywhere?"

"No, it didn't."

The wind had died down now, and except for the little yellow blob of the bedside lamp, the room was dark. The hooting of the taxis was infrequent, and what mind Peter had left to think with thought that it must be late at night. He was confused and wondered what he had been saying.

"Have I been talking much?"

"Yes. Quite a bit."

"Is it leading anywhere?"

"Is it leading *you* anywhere?" said the voice.

He could not tell. He lay back on the pillow and looked into the darkness. Three pinwheels came spinning toward him.

The intaglio led to nothing, and least of all to Shorty Cerwin, the little man who burned on Sing Sing's dread throne. What was the sequence of events, the chain of circumstance, that led you from the awkward little body of Julius Hassenpepper, lying flat on his face in the middle of his Park Avenue apartment, to the figure of Shorty Cerwin, the small and insignificant man who may or may not have fired the fatal slug from the .32-caliber Mauser automatic, but who, in the final go-round, confessed that he did, and then refused to say who was with him or if anyone was with him, declined to state who if anyone sent him or why he did it, declined to say anything at all that would help to uncover the facts behind the demise of a man who, as far as the world at large was concerned, was better off dead.

The chain of events which led to Shorty Cerwin was an elementary one. Simplicity itself. The little slug that ended Julius Hassenpepper's life was dug out of his evil brain by the autopsy surgeon and presented to the Homicide Bureau.

"Now all we have to do is to find the pistol that fired this slug," said Peter Hanley, "then find the person who owns the pistol."

"Check," said Inspector Battle.

There are a good many .32 automatic pistols in existence, and it is not too easy to find a particular one. At least not unless you can narrow the field.

In this case, the field was narrowed to the riff-raff who might be expected to kill a man for hire. Whoever killed Julius Hassenpepper pretty obviously was not the person who wanted him killed, but a person in the employ of someone who did. Someone evil enough, but not courageous enough, to do the thing himself, or herself.

Thus the trail led to the little man Shorty Cerwin.

He was picked up for something else. It started as a tavern brawl and, when Cerwin saw that he was outmatched by a longshoreman named Lars Larsen, he started for his room in the Plandome Hotel to get his equalizer. He was intercepted on the return trip by a radio car. They brought him, pistol and all, to the precinct house, and sent the pistol to the Homicide Bureau. There it was examined by Peter Hanley and Inspector Battle.

"This could be the one," Inspector Battle said.

Eventually the slug and the pistol were checked by the ballistics expert. His finding was conclusive. There was no doubt. This was the pistol that fired the slug that killed Julius Hassenpepper. Shorty Cerwin was brought before them. He was ragged and bruised, and besides all that, very nervous.

"You ain't got nothin' on me," he said.

"What makes you think we haven't?" asked Peter.

"All I did was have a fight with a guy named Larsen. I didn't kill nobody. What they got me in Homicide for?"

"That's the sixty-four-dollar question," said Peter.

The questioning was long and hard and relentless. At the end of it Shorty Cerwin was no longer nervous.

He was, in fact, exhausted.

"I done it," he admitted finally, his head resting on a battered desk. "I done it all right."

"Who else?" Peter asked. "Who was with you?"

"Nobody."

"Nobody at all? Not a girl?"

"A what? A girl? No."

His surprise seemed genuine, but still there was the story of Griselda Cunningham, and there was the intaglio lipstick holder.

"Nobody was with you the night you killed Julius Hassenpepper?"

"Leave me alone, will ya? I told you nobody was with me."

And that was all the little man ever said about it. He was questioned time after time, by the police and on the witness stand, but he never said anything more. Nothing about motive, or who paid him, or if anyone ever did, of whether anyone was with him. It was these things, and especially the brain that directed the finger, that bothered Peter Hanley.

It was in pursuit of this brain that he had run into Narcissa Maidstone on the stairway of the apartment house on Park Avenue. A tall blonde, cool as Mont Blanc, cool as they come.

She said, "You worked on the Hassenpepper case, didn't you?"

"Yes," he replied. He took a sip of her whisky. It was very good, although it could not be said of Peter Hanley that he was a judge of whisky; of race horses and women, perhaps, but not of whisky.

"Yes. I worked on it. Why do you ask?" He felt her eyes on him. "I don't usually like to mix business and pleasure," he said. "And so far this has been pleasure. Why do you want to know anything about the

Hassenpepper case?"

"I don't. I was just interested in your work."

Her cool green look went out the window.

But it was Narcissa Maidstone he must explain, it was she, not Shorty Cerwin, not Griselda Cunningham, not anyone else. Narcissa was at the center of the maze, his personal, obscure, dream-ridden maze. It was the killing of Narcissa that he must explain.

That was why he was here, meandering down the hot and gloomy avenues of his dreams; that was the reason. The reason and the question was: "Who killed Narcissa Maidstone?" She with the long flaxen hair twisted around her throat like Porphyria. Who did it? This was the manner in which Porphyria died, but Porphyria died not in reality but in a poem.

She died in a poem, and the manner of Narcissa's death was enough like hers to raise the question: was she killed by one who loved poetry and who decided in a moment of intoxication, of intoxication with her cool beauty and of Browning's lines, cold as the grave, to enact the verse?

> *I found*
> *A thing to do, and all her hair*
> *In one long yellow string I wound*
> *Three times her little throat around*
> *And strangled her. No pain felt she ...*

The lines were etched in fire in the darkness. The wind had risen a little, and it was cool in the room, but Peter felt hot and his throat was dry.

> *And all night long we have not stirred*
> *And yet God has not said a word!*

20

He sat bolt upright. The room was cool but he was hot and dry. He would have felt better if he could have broken out into a real sweat, but he was hot and dry as if in a fierce oven. The beautiful delicious languor of the barbiturate was gone; no longer did he float on a drifting cloud. It was the hangover again; but it was something more than a hangover. It was Fear. Fear. *Fear!*

The little flickering light inclined toward him.

"How are you feeling, Lieutenant Hanley?"

"I'm feeling bad. Very bad."

"In what way? Physically bad?"

"Yes. Physically bad. I feel lousy. And mentally, too. I feel lousy mentally."

"Could it be that you don't like the things you think?"

"It could be. And also some of the things I don't think. Can't think about. Can't quite remember."

"Such as the crucial question?"

"What is the crucial question?"

"Don't you know?"

"Yes. I know. I know what it is. Someone killed Narcissa Maidstone and the question is—the crucial question is—was it I?"

There was a silence. He saw the little blob of yellow light on the bedside table beside him and as his eyes came into a more normal focus he saw that there was no inclining candle flame, but Dr. Holmka, leaning slightly toward him, his finely molded head held to one side as he listened attentively.

"In a little while we shall give you some more medicine," said Dr. Holmka, "and you will be more comfortable."

"Thanks."

"How do you feel about things?"

"About what things?" Peter fumbled with his drug-clumsy hands for a cigarette, and Dr. Holmka helped him light it.

"All sorts of things," said Dr. Holmka. "About your progress. Do you think you are progressing?"

"I don't know. It's all a hell of a jumble. Some of the things I think—or dream—seem to be a hell of a jumble. But there are—what shall I say?— At times there are what I believe to be intimations of the truth."

"Very good," said Dr. Holmka. "When there are intimations of the truth, the truth is likely to be not far off."

Peter sank back on the pillow. He did not feel quite so dreadful as he had, but he still did not feel very good. The drug left a depressed and confused aftermath.

"Tell me," he said, "how long has this been going on? This amytal affair."

"Well," replied Dr. Holmka, "I should say that it is approximately half over."

"You mean it's the middle of the first night?"

"Yes."

"How am I doing?"

"How do you think you're doing?"

"Well, I've just told you. It's a jumble, but I get intimations of the truth. Maybe more will come. Tell me one thing. Do I talk much?"

"Quite a lot. Almost incessantly, in fact. Of course, we help you along a bit."

"How?"

"We ask you a question now and then, just to keep you going. Priming the pump, so to speak."

"What sort of questions?"

"Oh. Just questions. The questions are not important. The answers are."

They were silent for a few moments, then Dr. Holmka spoke very slowly: "It is nearly time for the medicine again. But first I should like it if we could piece together, while you are fully awake, what we have discovered so far. Are you too uncomfortable to do that?"

"No. I don't think so. You will have to do most of the piecing together anyway."

"Not necessarily. We shall both have to do it. You see"—and Peter felt that Dr. Holmka was smiling his courtly little Viennese smile—"this is rather an unusual case. We are interested in getting you well. That is our purpose, as doctors. But there is an added factor, of which you yourself are aware. There is pressure brought upon us from outside; we cannot merely keep you here and let nature take its course. We have to try to rush the process, and thus we find ourselves in the position of being detectives as well as doctors. Because at the heart of your problem—of your mental problem, your emotional problem—there is an unsolved murder.

"Your recovery hinges on the solution of this problem, which is in your own mind. It is there that the memories are locked, and there that the mystery will have to unfold itself. All the memories are there—no memory is ever really lost—and in the course of time they would come out. But we do not have that much time. We have only a very short period and during that period we must do our best. We cannot force these things very much, but we can force them a little. Is that clear?"

"Yes, very clear."

"Well, then. Let us just go over the ground."

"All right."

Peter found another cigarette and Dr. Holmka lighted it for him.

"Now, the first fact is this—the answer to this question. Why are you here?"

Peter felt dreadful, but he managed a wry grin. The question "Why are you here?" was almost the theme song of this institution. But Dr. Holmka repeated it as though it had never been asked before. "Why are you here? Do you know why you are here?"

"Yes. I know why I'm here."

"Why?"

Peter thought for a moment and then he chose his words as carefully as he could, picking them over to meet the precise attitude of Dr. Holmka, who did not seem to like flights of fancy. And while Peter thought about the words he was going to say, he also thought about Dr. Holmka, and how almost diabolically clever the man was. He asked the most innocuous questions, but he could ask them with great intensity, so that the patient got the feeling that behind them there lay answers with infinitely complex meanings.

And thus the simple little questions "How?" and "Why?" started the whole search backward.

You did it yourself, but you couldn't have done it all by yourself.

Again the question: "Do you know why you are here?"

"Yes."

"Then tell me," Dr. Holmka said. "In your own words."

Peter thought about the words again and then he said, "A girl named Narcissa Maidstone was murdered. I was found near the scene, talking out of my head. It looked as though—" He paused and began gathering the bedsheets in his fingers.

"Just say what's in your mind," Dr. Holmka prompted. "Everything. It is very important that you say everything that is in your mind."

Peter scowled and went on: "It looked as though I killed her. But—I couldn't really remember, and since I am a detective in the Homicide Bureau of the New York Police Department my friends had me brought here."

"Why?"

"Because they did not think I—" Peter began gathering up the bedsheets again.

"Go ahead. Please just say it."

"All right. Because they did not think I killed her."

"Did anyone think you killed Narcissa Maidstone?"

"Oh, yes. I expect quite a lot of people did."

"Who?"

"I don't know exactly. The District Attorney did, I guess. Maybe some of the top brass in the Police Department, too. Anyhow, the D.A. wants to arrest me and try me for murder."

"And you? What do you think? Do you think you killed her?"

Peter thought it all over for a moment, all the memories that he could find drifting around in the back of his mind, tried to get them all together and tie them up in a package that would hold the answer to everything. But he could not tie up his package; he could not get it all together in one piece.

"I don't know," he said at last. "At this moment I don't really know why I don't think I killed her. It's an impression—an impression more than anything else."

"An impression founded on what?"

"Founded on a feeling. Not thoughts, not ideas, not memories. Just a feeling. But that doesn't make any sense, does it?"

"Yes," Dr. Holmka said. "It makes sense to me."

"Then—what can I do? How can I go any farther than have?"

"That is why we are doing all this recapitulating," said Dr. Holmka. "We are going over what can be seen step by step. When we have done that, we will know better what cannot be seen. Is that correct?"

"Yes. That's right."

"What you have produced is a sketchy pattern. A kind of jigsaw puzzle. But that is all very well. We bring it out in bits and pieces, because what we are trying to learn is the content of your mind, for it is there that the secret of this—this mystery—is to be found. Is it not?"

"You were about to use the word *crime* instead of *mystery*, weren't you?" Peter asked.

"Ah. Perhaps I was."

"Why didn't you use it?"

Peter felt the little inclined light bend in the wind, then he thought the light was smiling faintly.

"Now it is you who are asking me questions," said Dr. Holmka. "Do you mind if I reply with a question of my own?"

"That's what I always expect of you."

"Then I shall ask: do you think the word *crime* is appropriate in this case?"

"Yes. Certainly. Don't you?"

"I am not so sure"—and now Dr. Holmka's voice seemed very distant—"but that the word *crime* should not be eliminated from the language, along with goodness and badness. For instance, what does badness mean to you? What is evil?"

Peter groped for ideas and words; behind his mind there was a picture, familiar from his many appearances in court, of a judge in black robes on the bench, above him the flag and before him the gavel. "Society feels ..." "It is the opinion of society ..." Other people's words echoed in his mind ...

"Badness is doing what hurts other people, I guess."

"Do you think bad people, as you say, are happy people?"

"No. Now that I think of it, I guess not. Not really."

"And do you think that unhappy people are well people or are they sick people?"

Peter Hanley listened to the wind for a moment. Then he said, "Sick people, mostly. I guess nearly always."

The little light wavered and seemed to smile faintly again.

"I am sorry for the digression," said Dr. Holmka. "But now you have an intimation of why I hesitate over such words as *crime*."

"Yes. I see."

"Now," Dr. Holmka went on quietly, "we will pursue the recapitulation only a moment longer, after which you can have some rest. I imagine that you must feel quite uncomfortable by now."

"I feel dreadful."

"Very well, then. You said you were here because a girl named Narcissa Maidstone was murdered. You were found near the scene under circumstances which indicated you might have committed the crime. You knew the girl, had indeed been with her about the time she was killed, but you could throw no real light as to your innocence or guilt. You had, as you said, blacked out, a condition which might have been one thing or another, and it might also have been what we, call a psychic block. Is that true so far?"

"Yes. That's all right as far as it goes." Peter was sitting up in bed now, with his eyes intent on Dr.

Holmka, who was poised in his slightly professorial attitude, his gold pen in his hand as though it were a pointer and he were lecturing a medical class. "Now, gentlemen, we will discuss anatomy. We will begin with the anatomy of Peter Hanley's mind. Here, you will see, is a little bump, a polyp. Inside this polyp will be found the secret of who killed Narcissa Maidstone ..."

"Are you going to sleep, Lieutenant Hanley?"

"Oh! No. By no means!"

"Well, then, by examining what you have said, what you have been thinking or dreaming or saying, we find that there are many areas of your memory which do not seem to touch directly on the matter of the death of Narcissa Maidstone. For example, there were childhood incidents, juvenile patterns. These help us to understand the kind of person you now are, but their bearing on the matter at hand, while of definite value, is remote.

"However, there is something that at first might seem unrelated but which, upon examination, may have a closer connection than seems evident to you. Lieutenant Hanley, permit me to ask you just one question and then I shall see that you are made comfortable so that you can get some rest. The question is this: Do you see any connection between the murder of Julius Hassenpepper and the death of Narcissa Maidstone?"

It was a question that Peter had never had put to him before, had never really asked himself. He thought about it for a while, listening to the wind rustle the curtains, hearing the nighttime hoots of the taxis.

"No, I don't see any connection at all. The only connection was that two people were—were killed."

The pen, like a golden pendulum, kept on swinging

in the lamplight.

"Just one more thing," said Dr. Holmka. "You once told us that Narcissa Maidstone was to you like a symbol, like a mountain in Montana you used to see from your barracks window: cool, distant, capped with snow—distant and unattainable. Do you think it possible that you never really knew Narcissa Maidstone, that she, too, was only a symbol, that when you looked at her you did not see her at all, but saw only something in your own mind? In short, is it not possible that there never was any such person as the Narcissa Maidstone whom you thought you knew, and that the real Narcissa Maidstone, who for a time inhabited your life and your dreams, might have been an entirely different kind of person from what you imagined her to be? Might, in fact, have had some connection with the Julius Hassenpepper murder? Do you think that to be possible?"

The gold-gleaming pendulum had paused as though illustrating a point in an anatomy lecture, but now it began swinging again. Peter watched it intently, the implications of the question seeping into the far corners of his mind, and at last he said:

"Yes. It is possible. Quite possible."

"Very well then."

Dr. Holmka rose and smiled faintly. The door shut behind him and in a few minutes Miss Lupino came in with the next shot of sodium amytal. When she too had gone Peter lay back and let the pleasant languor come over him. Now it was very quiet in the room. He switched off the light but then switched it on again. He did not want to be alone in the dark. Even the little blob of yellow lamplight made him feel less alone. The wind had died down again, and it was quiet. There was a most distant hum of the sleeping city.

21

He felt the delicious drowsiness of the drug; all his muscles were relaxed and he thought that in a moment he would be in a lovely deep sleep. And yet he fought to keep awake. He had noticed an odd thing in this clinic, under the effects of the sodium amytal. Sometimes he dreamed he was awake when actually he was fast asleep, and other times he had curious dreams when he was really awake.

And now he had the illusion that his mental processes were clearer, more lucid, more logical, and that everything appeared under a clear, cold light. He had been told he'd be likeliest to come upon the truth if he just let his mind wander, but now he did not want it to wander. Under this curious illusion of sharp mental clarity he wanted to try to think his way through his problem.

And yet, what was it he wanted to think about? Dr. Holmka had asked him, just before leaving, an immensely provocative question and it was this he had wanted to think about. But he could not remember what it was.

He was on the verge of going to sleep when suddenly it came to him, out of nowhere, as though etched in letters of fire. *Do you think you knew Narcissa Maidstone so little that you did not really see what she was like?*

It was this that he wanted to think out.

It was true that Narcissa was only a symbol to him. Now he could see that. He had always considered her elusive but now suddenly he saw that what he called her elusiveness was not, or might not have been, a quality pertaining to her at all. The something he could not find in her had nothing to do with her, really—and everything to do with him. And searching for it in her and not finding it, he thought of her as elusive, when it was not she, not really she, who was elusive, but the Holy Grail which all men seek and never find. Was that it?

He saw now that he never knew the real Narcissa.

And, since he had not known her really, could he find out now, in retrospect, what she was actually like? If he could do this, he might find himself on the road to unlocking the secret which had brought him here, and upon which his liberty, and possibly his sanity, depended. And what about the connection between the Julius Hassenpepper murder and the death of Narcissa? Was there such a connection? The reason Dr. Holmka had suggested this was that, in talking about Narcissa in his sodium amytal dream, he had also talked about the Julius Hassenpepper murder. Well, he had talked about other things, too, and surely there was no connection between all these things and the death of Narcissa. But there were a few things that were beyond the dreams.

For one thing, Narcissa's apartment was in the same building as Julius Hassenpepper's, and for another, it was there that he had first met her. Coming down the stairway he had met her, and she had known that he was a police officer and presumably she had known, too, that he had been working on the Julius Hassenpepper case. She had wanted to ask him something, and she had in fact asked him, but he could never remember precisely what it was.

But he had thought all this over a hundred times and always he had dismissed it at once. It was a coincidence only; a preposterous coincidence. And yet was it a coincidence? Could it have been that he had thought all along that Narcissa Maidstone had some connection with Julius Hassenpepper but that he had not wanted to think it? This was the direction in which Dr. Holmka was undoubtedly trying to lead him.

And her question—was it really an idle one, as he had thought?

At this moment the door swung open and Dr. Gatskill came in; Dr. Gatskill of the deep violet eyes, the bell-like tones, and the twinkling blue shoes.

"Oh," she said, "I'm surprised to find you awake. You are awake, aren't you?"

"Yes," Peter said. "Very much awake."

"Don't you think you ought to try to get some sleep? Aren't you sleepy?"

"Yes. I am. But I'm trying to think. I want to try to think."

Gatskill smiled faintly and sat down at the bedside. "In that case I'll only stay a minute. I'm not much interested in people who think. Don't you believe that thinking causes a lot of trouble?"

"I'm sure it does. But once in a while it seems to be necessary."

"What are you thinking about? Anything you'd like to tell me?"

Peter noticed that his tongue was getting thick again and he was having difficulty forming his words. He realized then that he would not be able to fight off the drug forever. His eyes were heavy, too, and the barbiturate spread through his arms and legs with a slow warm languor.

"Well, I was thinking about something Dr. Holmka said. He said—or rather suggested—that there might be a connection between the Julius Hassenpepper murder and the death of Narcissa Maidstone."

Dr. Gatskill gave him a long look. "That's very interesting. What do you think about that?"

"I don't know. That's really what I'm trying to think out. I had a feeling I was just beginning to get somewhere when you came in."

"I'm sorry," said Dr. Gatskill. "Shall I go out again?"

"No. It doesn't matter, actually. The fact is, I've gotten so sleepy that now I can't think anyway. I can't even talk anymore. You notice it, don't you, Doctor? My voice is funny. My eyes are getting funny, too." And they were indeed; something was wrong with the focus. Dr. Gatskill seemed to be receding into the distance, as though she were at the wrong end of a telescope. "There is something wrong with the focus, isn't there, Doctor?"

"No," she said, and he found that her voice was also a long way away. "I don't notice anything wrong, Lieutenant Hanley."

"The focus is very odd," he said, and closed his eyes. He caught a glimpse of God and Mrs. God in their tower looking over the ruin of the world. Then he heard the bell-like voice, a thousand miles away.

"I don't believe there is much use in trying to think, do you?" The voice was very clear and low, but very far off.

Peter said: "*Im Traum, ich geweinet.*"

"What did you say, Lieutenant Hanley?"

"I didn't say it. Heine said it. Heinrich Heine. 'In my dream, I have wept.'" He wondered whether she noticed this striking bit of erudition.

Three pinwheels danced in the darkness.

When you added up two and two, sometimes you got four and a half. Sometimes you got seven and one-eighth, if that was the size hat you wore. He was adding up two and two and, whatever it made, it didn't make four.

So the D.A. thought that he killed Narcissa Maidstone, and a lot of other people seemed to think so, too. Well, here was the thing, the theorem, the problem. You could not square the circle and two parallel lines would not meet. Excepting at infinity. But the point was, some people thought he had killed Narcissa Maidstone, and how did he, Peter Hanley, know that those people weren't right?

The only way in which two and two made four was thus and so: Narcissa Maidstone was dead. Strangled, in the manner of Porphyria, with her own flaxen hair wound round her lovely throat. That much added up. But after that the circle would not be squared.

The thing you had to get down to sooner or later was, who did it? If—as Inspector Battle seemed to think—he, Peter Hanley, didn't do it, who did? And here the mind began sliding along the grooves cut there by years of police work.

There were plenty of people who could have killed Narcissa. Her collection of characters was so vast, there were so many strange personalities floating around her, that it was almost impossible to consider all the possibilities. The thing was to try to be objective, to find a hilltop far away to stand on, and to eliminate Peter Hanley, at least for the present, from the picture. Once you got on that hilltop you began to look around and who and what did you find?

Well, Cal Sharkey. He was an odd enough and no doubt an unpleasant enough man to have done most anything, and yet when you got to thinking about him you saw that he didn't care two hoots for Narcissa Maidstone and how could you kill anybody you didn't care two hoots for?

Then there was that disbarred and discredited lawyer, Lance. Crowfoot Lance. Did he fit into the picture anywhere? If so, it was in some way that he, Peter Hanley, had no way of seeing or understanding. The fact was that Crowfoot Lance was in a class with Cal Sharkey and all the rest of the people who whirled around the perimeter of Narcissa Maidstone's life. They never really came close to her, never seemed really to touch her, any more than he, Peter Hanley, had been able to touch her. Of all the people around her it was impossible to find anyone close enough to her to have killed her. Except him, Peter Hanley. He was the closest. And, after all was said and done, the likeliest.

And yet this Crowfoot Lance matter opened up a tiny little crack in the doorway which Dr. Holmka seemed to be trying to get him to open. Crowfoot Lance, a known henchman of Julius Hassenpepper, was with Narcissa Maidstone on Fifth Avenue one day. This was a thing that led the way Dr. Holmka seemed to be trying to point.

Was this the way his mind had to go and did not want to go? Had he been trying not to see this and must he now make himself see it?

He did not know. Thinking was hard work anyway, and he had been advised against it. Bad for the constitution. He broke the triangle into sixteen thousand infinitesimal bits and scattered them out the window. They fell among the roses. And he sailed the unsquared circle all the way across Manhattan. It stuck on the tip of the Chrysler Tower.

Sergeant Quinlan squinted down his nose. "So you want to be a cop, do yez?"

It was a summer afternoon, Peter was fifteen years old, and they were sitting on a pier at the foot of Old

Catherine Slip watching the river traffic.

"Yes, I do." Peter was half on the defensive, and for a very good reason. He had spent much of his young life disobeying, taunting, eluding, defying, and sometimes fighting the cops, and so he hardly knew with what derision his choice of a career would be met.

"Well," said Sergeant Quinlan, "being a cop is better than being a cop-fighter." He squinted into the gray dazzle of the gray river between them and Brooklyn. "As a matter of fact," he added, "you started out like you was going to be a cop-fighter. But you got better stuff'n that in you. I know you since you was knee-high, and I known your ma, too, and you ain't no born cop-fighter."

Sergeant Quinlan gave his stick another twirl and, still squinting into the gray river, he said, "I'll tell you something about cop-fighters, too, Pete. It don't get them nowhere. I guess they feel good for a while—they think they're bigger 'n' stronger 'n the law, but to tell you the truth, most cop-fighters I ever knew ended up in Sing Sing. Or some place like that.

"And I'll tell you something about cops, too. It may look to you like there's a lot of crooked ones, but they're just the ones you hear about. Most all cops is decent, and they ain't no more important job than a cop's job. It ain't all pinchin' people and packin' 'em off to the station house. A cop on a beat has got just as big a job as a judge."

Sergeant Quinlan spat into the East River, and said again, "In its way, it's just as big a job as a judge on a bench."

They just stood there, looking at the gray gleam of the summer sun on the East River, and a tug came wallowing past them, bucking the outgoing tide. At the same time there was a puff of wind and they were suddenly overwhelmed by the redolence of the Fulton Street fish market.

22

There was a smoky blue sofa and the girl Narcissa Maidstone was sitting on it. She gave him her cool stare and said, "I like being with you, copper. You're nice."

"Yes? Why? Also how?"

"Oh. I don't know. You just are, that's all. I'm surprised."

"What surprises you?"

"I'm surprised to learn that your kind of a guy is a cop."

"It really shouldn't surprise you at all. Lots of kinds of guys are cops. I very nearly went into the priesthood, and then when I didn't, I studied law. Good thing for a cop to know. A good cop knows as much as he can about everything."

"Everything?"

"Lots of things."

Narcissa rose from the sofa, lighted a king-size cigarette with a gold tip, and walked to the window, a spacious window with expensive drapes overlooking one of Park Avenue's plushiest sections. Every inch of the street was paved with gold. You couldn't see it but it was there—the gold was in the rentals and in the tax rate.

Narcissa, smoking her king-size cigarette, was a king-size girl and she lived in a king-size apartment. He guessed that was why he wanted her. He was on the make, on the way up, and he wanted something flashy and expensive to show for it. She was no doubt a symbol of other things, deeper and more obscure things, but she was also a symbol of the kind of success he saw for himself. Success with a capital S, the mad Manhattan success. A Cadillac convertible and a flaxen blonde with cool green eyes—this was what his kind of guy wanted to show the world.

But that was not what he thought. What he thought was how he wanted her, and how, like a dream or a soap bubble, he could never really catch her.

"You know," she said, returning from the window, "I don't think I'm good for you, really. Believe me."

"You're talking through your hat."

"No, I'm not. I mean it. Sometimes I think I'm not really your type."

"What is my type?"

"Oh"—she made a wide gesture with her long cool fingers—"I don't know exactly. Somebody warmer than I am, I guess. I'm not really very warm, you know."

"You suit me, baby." He took her in his arms and she gave him that cool faraway kiss, like the far-off snow-topped mountains. Like Mount LoLo, cool, distant, not really there.

Suddenly she broke away and went to the window again in quick long strides, turned swiftly and faced him. There were tears in her eyes.

"Please. Please let's not do that again!"

"Why not?"

She bit her lip. "I don't want to."

"Don't you like it?"

"Yes."

"Then—"

She tossed her head; he thought the gesture expressed defiance.

"We mustn't. We just mustn't go on. Someday I'll explain."

He looked at her in silence for a moment. "Some other guy, I presume. Dr. Livingstone, I presume."

"No, no. It isn't that. If it were, I'd tell you. But it isn't. Now go away, will you? Please go away."

Her eyes, no longer wet, seemed full of fear. What could she be afraid of?

"I want to stay," he said.

"No. Please don't. Please don't stay!" She drew in a sharp little breath. "Look. You think I've been giving you the runaround. Maybe I have. I haven't been very good to you. You don't deserve it this way. But there's a reason why we can't go on. There's a big reason and there's a lot of little things. You're a square guy and you deserve the truth. I'm going to tell you everything. But not now. Please, not now. Now go away, will you? Please go away."

He wanted to stay, but he didn't. In such matters a woman's word is the law. He went out and walked the streets, because she had made him unhappy and he couldn't tell why. He really couldn't tell why.

He was sitting in the Homicide Bureau with his feet on the desk and Inspector Battle was sitting opposite him.

"You don't look happy, son. What's gone wrong?"

Peter took out his .38-caliber pistol, ejected all the cartridges, and began cleaning the mechanism, as he did at least once every day.

"Nothing's wrong."

"You haven't seemed right since you finished the Hassenpepper case," said Inspector Battle. "I can understand how you feel, but it don't pay to think about these things. It isn't the first time we didn't get the real killer. We got one of them and that was the best we could do. Maybe the rest of it will turn up someday. Don't worry about it."

"I'm not worrying about it." Peter pulled a dry rag through the barrel and it came out slightly smudged with oil.

Inspector Battle studied him, squinting. "No? A babe, then. I might have figured it was a babe."

Peter did not answer.

"That nightclub girl, I guess," said Inspector Battle.

Peter ran the rag through once more, stuck a square of paper against the cocked hammer, squinted down the barrel. It was clean as a whistle; the lands of the rifling gleamed against the shadows of the grooves.

Inspector Battle leaned forward. "How did you get mixed up with her in the first place, Peter?"

"I'm not mixed up with her."

"Well, have it your own way. You're not mixed up with her. Anyway, how did you meet her?"

"While I was cleaning up the Hassenpepper case."

"I thought so."

Peter reloaded the pistol, shut the chamber, and laid it on the scarred desk in front of him. He tilted himself back in his chair. A wave of resentment surged over him.

"What do you mean, you thought so?"

Inspector Battle looked at his pipe. "That girl knows a lot of people," he said. "All kinds of people."

"Well? So what? She's an entertainer. She's supposed to know all kinds of people. That's her business."

"I know all that, but that's not exactly what I mean. What I mean is that she knows too many of the wrong kind of people."

Peter checked the safety catch on the pistol and, holding it at arm's length, sighted on the portrait of DeWitt Clinton which, for some reason or another, hung on the far wall. He got the front sight right between the eyes.

"What's all this to you, anyway? When you come right down to it, I don't see how it concerns you."

Inspector Battle began packing his pipe with the rough strong tobacco to which he was addicted. "Maybe you haven't noticed it," he said slowly, "but in my own mind I always thought I was your friend."

Peter laid down the pistol. "I always thought you were, too. I still do. That's why I'm a little surprised at this—at this—"

"Prying? Meddling?"

"I didn't say that."

"No. You didn't exactly say that."

Inspector Battle began puffing his pipe, and big clouds of blue smoke began to ascend in the direction of DeWitt Clinton.

"It's because I'm your friend that I got a little worried when you began to have girl trouble. Everybody has girl trouble once in a while and it could happen to you as well as the next guy. But when I found out who the girl was it was different."

"What do you mean?"

"Just what I said. I've done quite a lot of checking around on this—this Narcissa Maidstone as she calls herself. In fact, I wondered why you hadn't come up with the same conclusions about her. I guess they're right when they say love is blind."

Peter took up his pistol again and aimed it at the point of DeWitt Clinton's chin.

"What conclusions?"

"While you were looking the other way, this girl was in the company of a vast assortment of characters who are not what I would call New York's finest citizens."

"Such as who?" Peter opened the chamber of his

pistol again and, releasing the safety catch, began snapping the trigger.

"Such as, for instance, a lot of hangers-on of Julius Hassenpepper. She was extra friendly with too many of them."

"In the nightclub business you meet everybody."

"Yes," Inspector Battle said slowly. "I expect you do. And I expect she did."

The hammer of Peter's revolver fell with a sharp little click and Inspector Battle, with an almost imperceptible start, followed the aim to the portrait of DeWitt Clinton. Then, blowing a final thick cloud of smoke in the direction of the picture, he knocked out the pipe against his square-toed shoes and began in his methodical way to reload it.

"I suppose you do meet everybody. But that doesn't mean you necessarily have to live with everybody."

The pistol snapped with its evil little click and Peter laid it down on the desk again.

"What did you say?"

"I said you didn't necessarily have to live with everybody, even if you are a nightclub singer."

"I don't like that," said Peter.

"I didn't expect you to."

"I would just as soon we didn't talk about it any further."

Inspector Battle began puffing blue clouds of smoke again. "I'm not going to talk about it much further, but there are a couple more things I have to say. I wouldn't have brought the subject up at all if I hadn't thought it was necessary to keep you out of trouble. The fact is, I began checking up on this girl from the very beginning, over a year ago, when you first met her. Or she met you, whichever it was. It was too close to the windup of the Hassenpepper case. And you were worn out. You didn't know it, but you weren't really in your right mind. You needed a vacation. You needed a rest a lot more than you needed Narcissa Maidstone. But I didn't say anything. But now I have to. Things have developed quite enough, and besides, I finally got an order about it."

"You got a what?"

"An order. I got an order to give you a kind of quiet warning."

"Yes? Who from?" Peter began putting the cartridges back in the chamber, one by one. Then he slammed shut the chamber, set the safety catch, and slid the pistol into his shoulder holster.

Inspector Battle leaned forward with the squarish pipe again between his fingers.

"I'll tell you where it came from," he said. "It came from the Chief. And I'll also tell you where I think he got it. From the Commissioner."

"The Commissioner!"

"Yes. The Commissioner. I have an idea that's where it began—in the Commissioner's office."

"I don't get it. Why should the Commissioner bother his head about the babes I go out with?"

Inspector Battle blew a large cloud of smoke into the already murky air. "It doesn't seem to percolate into your dumb young skull that the Commissioner has many friends in all walks of life. And it also doesn't seem to percolate into your skull that perhaps one of the Commissioner's friends is one of Narcissa's friends."

"I don't believe it," said Peter Hanley.

"You remember you bumped your head against the Commissioner's office once before," said Inspector Battle. "That time you tried to hang the murder of Hacko Judson on to Julius Hassenpepper."

"That wasn't the Commissioner. That was George Scott."

"Who knows who it was? It was the Commissioner's office."

"I still don't believe it."

"You don't want to believe it."

"No. I don't want to believe it." He got up, tugged at the shoulder holster to get it adjusted under his coat, jammed his hat down over his eyes, and went out, slamming the door. DeWitt Clinton stared fiercely after him.

23

It was April, and evening, and there was a chill wind in the air. Winter was reaching out, in her death throes, into the domain of spring. Peter Hanley, walking in the direction of Foley Square with the East River at his back, seethed and boiled. His head was on fire from his confused anger.

He had no idea where he was going, what he wanted to do. His instinct was that of an animal, hurt beyond endurance, without means or power to fight back.

He thought that he was angry at the Inspector, but how could he be angry at the Inspector? Inspector Battle was his friend. Was it the Chief then? The Commissioner? Was it Narcissa?

And then he knew. He was angry because he had been told the truth, and the truth he could not face. What did you do with a truth such as this?

How did you deal with it, really? You had been deeply in love with a girl, cool and beautiful as the snow-tipped mountain tops, you had seen in her everything you wanted, ever dreamed about, you had pinned your whole life on her, as though she were a goddess; and then suddenly she appeared to you, or was revealed to you, as something quite common, too common—and false, as well. So what did you do? Get mad? Get mad at the person who told you the truth?

But why did Inspector Battle's remarks about Narcissa produce such a complicated reaction in him? Was it that he had come to identify Narcissa with himself, so that an attack on her constituted an attack on him? Or was it merely that, deep within him, he had already known that what Inspector Battle had said was true?

But was it true? Perhaps it wasn't true at all.

Yet his heart and soul and mind told him that it was. She was no good. Narcissa Maidstone was no good. She was not on the level and she was not what he had supposed her to be, had wanted her to be. His goddess lay broken in the dust, the goddess of the jade-green look and the burnished flaxen hair lay in the dust.

And, although he himself had created this image, and she was in no way to blame for the destruction of the illusion, it was against her that his anger was directed. It was she whom he blamed, whom he wished to punish. He was hurt and he wanted to hurt back.

He had a blind desire to hurt back.

He stopped on the next corner and hailed a cab.

"Park Avenue," he said. "Let me off near the Armory."

He found her in the apartment sitting at the piano, rehearsing a new song, a simple little ditty called "Say It Forever", and it made the Hit Parade and was on everybody's lips for a month or two after that. On everybody's lips, that is, but Narcissa's. She never sang it again.

The words went:

> *Say it again,*
> *Say it forever.*
> *Say you love me,*
> *Can't do without me,*
> *Nobody else will do:*
> *Say it again,*
> *Say it forever.*

There was a breath-catching little melody that went with it.

Peter waited, standing, until she had finished, and then she crossed the room to greet him.

"Why, hello, copper. What brings you here? You look sort of strange. What's bothering you?"

She sat down on the sofa and he sat opposite her. She lighted one of her long king-size cigarettes with the gold tips, and he rolled himself a cigarette with a brown cigarette paper.

"Like a drink? Or coffee?" she asked.

"Nothing, thanks."

He really did not know what he wanted to say.

What he said was: "What I'd like to know is why you've been giving me the runaround." He did not know what he was going to say, but that was what he said, indelicately, inelegantly, and choked with tension.

"What did you say?" Her eyes were wide and cool but the hostility came through.

He put his cigarette down in the cloisonné ash tray on the little coffee table. His gesture was very deliberate.

"I want to know why I never get anything but the runaround from you. Why you are never on the level. Tell me."

"Make yourself clearer."

"You knew how I felt about you, didn't you?"

"Well, yes, I think I did. You've always been very flattering."

"It was not my intention to flatter you." He picked up the remains of his brown-paper cigarette and ground it to bits. "To put it plainly, I was in love with you. You knew that. Whatever being in love is, I don't know, but that's what it was, and you knew it."

Narcissa made a quick impatient gesture with her long slim hand. "Look, if there's something on your mind, get it off."

He began to roll another cigarette, but all the tobacco spilled out. His words did likewise.

"I don't like the crowd you go around with," he said, stabbing out in the first direction that he could think of. "They certainly don't reflect very handsomely on your taste or judgment."

She gave him a long cool surveying look, but the hostility in her eyes was deeper. "You never said that before. What's got into you now? Why didn't you say so sooner?"

"I'm saying so now. Anyhow, what would you have done about it if I had?"

"Nothing, nothing at all."

"That's what I thought."

"Look," she said, and there was a biting edge on her words, "I asked you to get off your mind whatever you had on it. Now let's get it off so we can forget it."

"It isn't going to be anything we can forget so easily."

"Well, get it off anyway. I don't like you much when you're in this kind of a mood."

"I didn't expect you to," Peter said. He picked up one of her gold-tipped, king-size cigarettes, started to light it, then put it down again, unlit. "I want to ask you a question."

"All right. Ask it."

"Did you ever know Julius Hassenpepper?"

"No."

"Did you ever know anyone who did know him?"

"No." She looked straight at him but he thought she was lying. "I thought you didn't like talking business with me."

"I didn't. I still don't. But I'm doing it. I'm trying to find out something about you and me."

"I always did think you were a little screwy. Now you're convincing me. Do you carry these murder cases around in your head all the time?"

"Yes," he said. "As a matter of fact, I do."

Peter leaned back in the chair, stretching his legs out in front of him. Now that he was talking he was beginning to relax and the true emotion began to come out—not fear, or depression, or anxiety, or anything frustrated or complicated. It was anger. Pure anger. He wanted to hurt her and when he had finished hurting her he wanted never to see her again. Never again, never anywhere on the face of the earth.

He spoke very slowly and very softly: "I think you are lying about Julius Hassenpepper."

She stared at him. She said nothing, but the red came up in her cheeks.

"And now," he said, "I'm going to ask you one, more question. Do you know Anthony Marriner, the Police Commissioner? And if so, how well?"

She stood up quickly, stamping her feet, and the flaxen hair fell tumbling down about her shoulders. Her face was scarlet and the green in her eyes was a green fire.

"Yes," she said, her voice low but electrical with repressed emotion, "I do know Anthony Marriner. I've known him a long time. What's it got to do with you?"

"Nothing. At least nothing any longer. Yesterday, yes. Today, no."

"A cop," she said, with a warning edge on her voice, "ought to be very careful before getting mixed up on the wrong side of Anthony Marriner."

"Because he's the Police Commissioner? Yes, I can see that. But I never got mixed up with him until just now. And I still don't quite know how or why."

"I'll tell you how and why," Narcissa said. "Anthony Marriner was a very good friend of mine. He got me my start. He did everything for me."

"And you did everything for him?"

"I guess you mean that as a nasty crack. But it doesn't make any difference. I gave Anthony Marriner everything he wanted. Why shouldn't I have? Yes, I lived with him. It was after his divorce and he needed me. I'm not ashamed of it. Why should I be, and why should you bring it up anyway? What's it to you?"

"It isn't anything to me anymore. Nothing you did or do or ever will do is anything to me. Not now. I just want to know, that's all. Just getting the facts straight. One more question and then I'm finished."

"Thanks."

"Are you still sleeping with Anthony Marriner?"

"No." The answer was short, explosive, defiant. Peter was sure she was lying. They were silent for a long time, then suddenly she moved toward him and put a long cool hand on his forehead.

"Look, I'm sorry. I see how upset you are and I guess it could have been my fault. I told you once before that I was no good for you and I'm telling you again. I intended to try to explain something to you, and then never see you again. But you've made it pretty hard."

"I don't want you to explain anything. It doesn't matter."

There was the distant chiming of the doorbell, and the pattering footsteps of Minnie, Narcissa's maid, could be heard on the way. Automatically Narcissa got a compact out of the white suede handbag beside her. He had never seen it before but he had seen something like it. It was a very expensive gold compact, and on its side was an intaglio plaque, showing the head of Diana, Goddess of the Hunt.

Minnie came in hesitantly, shutting the door as she came, but as soon as she had shut the door it opened again. Someone was coming in behind her.

24

Three pinwheels came out of the darkness. The wind came out of the darkness, too; out of the sea and the East River and out of the deep canyons of Manhattan. It came and rustled the curtains of Peter's windows. It rustled with little clicking sound, a sound like the death rattle.

But Peter did not hear. He heard only the bell-like tone of a distant voice. A voice that said, "Yes. I heard what you said. You said the girl took out a compact with an intaglio design of the Goddess Diana on the side. Is that important to you?"

He could hear his own voice. It was strangled, almost inarticulate, like a voice in a nightmare.

"Yes, it's important. The intaglio is very important. Intaglio means etched, Doctor. Etched. That's deep; it goes deep."

The bell-like tones said something but they were too distant for him to hear.

"A door opened," he said. "Do you understand that. Doctor? A door opened."

"Yes. I understand."

"The door opening is very important, very significant. It is, symbolic of something. The door opened and it has some meaning."

"Yes? Who came in?"

"I don't know. I don't know who came in. The light went out. That, too, is important, but I don't just know why. The light went out just after the door opened. Because then the door closed again and the light was out."

"Who came in?"

"I don't know. The light went out."

The voice said something else, but this he did not hear, because the three pinwheels came out of the darkness again. They made a whirring sound.

The door opened and the light went out.

But before the light went out he saw the look on Narcissa's face. It was quite drained of color, all but the scarlet lips, and the green eyes were wide with fright. She said nothing, the scarlet lips said nothing.

The door opened and someone came in.

The maid screamed. Peter heard her running. Narcissa screamed. She did not run.

Peter sensed the movement of someone, the unknown someone, in the darkness. He blocked the body with his own body. Two bodies went down in a tangle in the darkness, flailing arms, flailing legs. Strong fingers were against his throat. He broke their grip. The two bodies rolled across the floor and a vase crashed in a splinter of sharp sound.

Then they were up and Peter was lunging at a shadow. The shadow spun into the corner with a crash. But then the shadow was up again, was upon him. The shadow overpowered him, like the shadow in a nightmare. They went down again, and a coffee table went over with a sharp crack. The nightmare had strong brutish fingers. They tightened around Peter's throat. They pressed against his windpipe and Peter fought for his life. He tried to get his pistol out of the shoulder holster, but the nightmare was across his chest and he could not move. The pressure on his windpipe increased. He struggled, kicked, tried to bite. But the pressure became stronger and the darkness of the room melted into a greater darkness.

"Porjie!" Narcissa cried. Then the darkness closed in and pinwheels danced back and forth against a curtain of velvet.

There was a long time of the darkness, a long time when he could not remember. And when he came to there was nothing but darkness and silence. He got up from the darkness and switched on a light. And when he could see, he saw the one sight that was not to fade from his mind, ever.

Narcissa, the lovely cool Narcissa, lay sprawled on the sofa, with her long flaxen hair wound around her white throat. The waxen curve of her breast showed, but all the passion—all the possible passion, all the sensuousness—was gone. Narcissa was a figure in wax. The eyes, the green jade eyes that had so fascinated him, stared at the ceiling. Narcissa was dead.

Peter staggered to the door, down the carpeted stairs, and out into Park Avenue. It was dark.

Peter sat bolt upright. He was sweating and miserable but he knew that he had to leave this place at once. But the clear bell-like voice—not so distant now—arrested him, would not let him go.

"The intaglio compact?" the voice said. "It means

something to you, doesn't it?"

"It means everything!" Peter's voice was strangled and hoarse. "It means everything!"

"Why?"

"Because it was a clue to all the loose ends in the Hassenpepper case!" Peter exclaimed. "Even in my confused state of mind I saw that. And that's why, when I came back with the policeman, and while we waited for the detectives from the station house, I looked for the compact. It was the only really conscious thing I did. But it wasn't there. The compact was not there when we came back. I wanted it, don't you see, because there could have been only one set of that kind, and the companion piece—the lipstick holder—was found near Julius Hassenpepper's body. We traced the .32-caliber Mauser bullet to Shorty Cerwin but we never traced the lipstick holder to anyone."

Peter swung his legs out of the bed and sat staring at Dr. Gatskill. The quiet violet eyes looked back at him beneath the lamplight and the low clear voice came back.

"And then you traced it to Narcissa. Why do you suppose you had never seen her with it before?"

"I don't know. It was probably by accident that she let me see it. She was very excited when the doorbell rang."

"Do you think it possible," Dr. Gatskill asked slowly, "that she let you see it deliberately? As a warning?"

"What?" Then the meaning of this seeped slowly into his mind, and at last he said, "Yes. That's possible. That's quite possible."

They were silent for a moment while Peter tried to gather up all the scattered thoughts, the jumbled memories that were beginning to emerge. The bell-like voice came softly again.

"Do you think that the reason you could not remember was that your seeing Narcissa with the intaglio compact was a tremendous shock in your mind?"

"Yes, I suppose so. That was one reason." Then he added, "Of course, being half-choked to death didn't do my mental faculties any good, either."

"But the real shock—the deep shock—may have been when you saw something that linked the girl you idealized to the murder of Julius Hassenpepper. Do you think that might be so?"

The room was very quiet and outside it was very quiet, too. The question hung in the air. Was it this shock that had frozen his mental processes and made it impossible for him to remember the things he had needed to remember?

Suddenly Peter Hanley covered his face with his hands. "Yes, I suppose it was that. As simple—and as complicated—as that."

Dr. Gatskill made a slight movement. "Do you think you are any nearer the solution of your problem?"

"Yes.

"Do you have any idea about leaving here?"

Peter thought for a moment.

"I should like to go as soon as possible. There are some things I must check at once." Then he added, "But what do you think?"

"It is really up to you," she said. "Why don't you go for a day or so, and see how it works out? Will that give you enough time?"

"Yes. That would be enough. I haven't remembered everything. But I have remembered a good many things."

"It doesn't do any good to hide from your memories, does it?" Dr. Gatskill asked quietly.

"No," said Peter.

Dr. Gatskill rose.

"By the way," she said, "do you remember mentioning that Narcissa, in the dark room, before she was killed, cried out the name 'Porjie'?"

"Yes. I remember that."

"Who is Porjie?"

"I don't know. That is one of the things I am going to find out."

"I am sure you are." She turned to leave. He stopped her.

"Dr. Gatskill—"

"Yes?"

"I think I ought to leave today. This morning."

"Do you? Well, I suppose it's really up to you. I'll have a talk with Dr. Holmka and we'll let you know."

"I must leave!" Peter said fiercely.

"Why?"

"Because the end of the road is not in this hospital. It is somewhere else."

She smiled faintly. "Are you still searching for the unknown—or for the intaglio compact with the Goddess Diana on it?"

"Both," he said.

She put her hand on the door knob. "I think you can plan on leaving later in the morning. We will discontinue the heavy medication and just give you something light. So you won't feel so dreadful."

"Thanks. I won't need anything. I feel all right."

"Something off your mind?"

"A little."

She went out the door with a flash of starched gown and a twinkle of blue shoes. He could hear her going down the corridor and opening the door of the nurse's office.

Peter put his feet under the sheets and lay back. The September dawn was coming over Manhattan, sharp and clear, with an intense blue sky. After a while Miss Lupino came and gave him some medicine in a little capsule.

"No more sodium amytal?" he asked.

"No. No more for you. But this will help you feel comfortable."

On First Avenue a taxi horn announced the new day and on the East River the hoarse voice of a tug replied. And while the dawn came up, Peter Hanley slept.

25

Peter slept lightly. A great weight seemed to have been lifted from his mind and for the first time since he had been in the Whitman-Bourne Clinic he felt almost happy. What he felt was that all the doors that had been shut were now about to be opened.

There were the early morning noises, of which he was only partly aware, and the deep breathing of other patients which he could hear issuing from their rooms and dorms along the corridor.

At seven o'clock he heard footsteps and his eyelids parted slightly and he was vaguely aware of the twinkle of blue shoes in his drowsy gaze.

"Your temperature," a voice said softly.

"What? Still that?" he murmured and smiled faintly but did not really wake up. None the less the thermometer was inserted between his lips.

He lay back drowsily, with the thermometer stuck out at a cocky angle from his mouth. For the first time since he had been in this place he had a feeling of assurance, of power. It wasn't that he had remembered everything in crystal clear detail. But he had remembered enough to begin to get to work. What was necessary now was that old routine he knew so well—the painstaking checking of detail.

He heard a sound, a sound he had learned to recognize and this time he opened his eyelids wider and his gaze, though drowsy still, did not stop at the blue shoes but went up—up—and he saw it was Miss Dibble standing there. Miss Dibble in blue shoes. She had a hypodermic and the customary little box of ampules marked *Sodium Amytal*, and the click of the shoes was the sound that had been familiar.

"Hey!" Peter cried out, his mind searching for something in alarm, seeking to latch onto something elusive. "No more of that. I'm not supposed to have any more of that!"

Miss Dibble raised her eyebrows. "Are you giving the orders around here now?" she asked, busying herself with the hypodermic.

"But—but," said Peter, "I'm leaving today. No more knockout drops. No more sodium amytal. Didn't Dr. Gatskill tell you?" A bell was ringing in his mind ... Miss Dibble ... blue shoes ...

"It's all right, everything's all right now, Lieutenant Hanley," Miss Dibble said in her most infuriatingly soothing tones. She approached his bed, the hypodermic upraised.

Peter tried to move but his arm was heavy, his limbs leaden.

"Just be quiet now," said Miss Dibble. And before he could jerk away she grasped his arm and the needle went smoothly and deftly under the skin of his forearm.

"What are you trying to do?" Peter pulled away now,

sweating, but he was too late. He had the full dose of the stuff flowing through his veins.

"There," said Miss Dibble with a self-satisfied and rather grim look. "You'll be quiet now."

She picked up her equipment and went quickly out of the room.

Peter started to rise, to try to follow her, but he suddenly realized that this was no ordinary dose of amytal. She must have made a mistake, given him too much, given him the wrong medicine. He didn't know. He knew that he was overpowered, smothered, and he had a panicky sensation that he was choking to death. He fought for breath, fought to cry out, but he was paralyzed.

He was able to get half out of bed, and then he fell back. A blackness began to envelop him, but then he managed to open his eyes and he was aware that again someone was in the room. He caught a glimpse of a starched skirt and a pair of blue shoes going out of the door, and the choking sensation returned.

Then he was lying on his bed and he heard Dr. Gatskill's voice. "The intravenous caffeine is bringing him around."

He opened his eyes. Dr. Gatskill was standing beside his bed, and Dr. Holmka, and also a young doctor whom he had never seen before. He was holding a hypodermic needle in his hand.

"Not that!" Peter muttered. "I've had all the shots I ever want."

"You very nearly had one too many," Dr. Gatskill said, her voice filled with concern. "You had a strong enough solution of sodium amytal to have killed an ordinary man. You are lucky to have a strong constitution. And lucky we found you quickly enough to bring you out of it."

"Miss Dibble—she did it. She gave me the stuff. I told her not to. Where's Miss Dibble?"

"That's what we should all like to know," said Dr. Holmka in his clipped precise voice. "Miss Dibble has disappeared."

"Disappeared!" Peter raised himself up on the edge of the bed. He felt dreadful but now his head was fairly clear. "I think she deliberately tried to kill me."

"It might interest you to know," said Dr. Gatskill quietly, "that she applied for work after you came here. She is a psychiatric nurse and psychiatric nurses are scarce. Her credentials were good and the clinic employed her. She managed to get herself assigned to your floor by claiming she hadn't yet got over an experience with a violent patient. What her connections outside the hospital are—we don't know. Perhaps you know."

Peter hesitated, and passed his hand over his aching head. "There's some connection. I'll add it up when I get out of here."

"How do you feel?"

"Terrible."

"Perhaps you had better not leave today. You had a close shave."

"I'll be all right. Some breakfast and a little black coffee and I'll be perfectly okay. I must go. I really must go today."

"Well—" She looked at Dr. Holmka.

"He's tough," said Dr. Holmka. "I daresay he'll be all right."

And Dr. Gatskill turned and gave Peter a smile which seemed to be made of tenderness and compassion.

It seemed a little odd to be sitting once again in the

Homicide Bureau. He was still shaky from the aftereffects of the amytal overdose but otherwise he felt all right. He put his feet on the desk and relaxed.

Inspector Battle took out the familiar squarish pipe and began turning it over and over again in his squarish fingers. "Of course, once the D.A. learns you're out of that place he isn't going to need any habeas corpus."

"No," said Peter. "The body is already here."

"On the other hand," Inspector Battle went on, "if all the things you have told me are true and we can prove them, then it won't matter whether he gets a habeas corpus or not. We'll have the handcuffs on somebody else."

"Right."

Inspector Battle began loading his pipe. Peter saw that the whaling-parson eyes were studying him, cautiously, shrewdly. Obviously, the inspector was still wondering if Peter was still off his rocker. And if so, how far off.

"It's a fairly fantastic idea you have," Inspector Battle said at last. "I hope you know what you're doing."

"I don't, altogether. But I have a good idea. Now what did you do about the maid? Minnie."

"The boys are working on it. But if she was in on it, she may be hard to catch."

"She won't be hard to catch because of fear of us," Peter said. "But because of fear of the other people."

"It doesn't make any difference what she's afraid of, she'll be hard to catch. She might even be at the bottom of the river. In which case she'll do us no good whether we catch her or not."

"You're a chronic pessimist," Peter said.

"All right. You hope for the best and I'll be the pessimist."

"That suits me. And now what do you say we get moving?"

"I'm still waiting for a report on the Dibble woman," the inspector said. "Besides, there's nowhere to move. We haven't got enough evidence."

"We could take a chance."

"Like what?"

"Let's start by going to the Commissioner's office."

Inspector Battle set down his pipe in alarm. "If the Commissioner sees you round there, he'll have you locked up. He's just as anxious to do it as the D.A. It would be a mistake to go there."

"I'm hoping for the best," Peter said. "We've got to start somewhere and it might as well be there. If we sit around much longer I'll be locked up anyway."

"We can't do it. We haven't got enough to go on."

"Come on." And Peter started out the door, and as he did so he drew an imaginary bead right between the eyes of DeWitt Clinton.

26

Anthony Marriner's office was in the big gilt-domed Municipal Building and they didn't have much trouble getting past the small brass and the medium brass and into the inner sanctum. That is, into the outer ring of the inner sanctum, where sat the Commissioner's Executive Secretary, George Scott.

He eyed them carefully, as befitted the watchdog of an important official, and said, "Sit down, gentlemen. The Commissioner isn't in. Would you care to wait? I think he's at a meeting of the Board of Estimate."

"We're kind of a board of estimate ourselves," said Peer. He made a circle round the room, looked into the inner office of the Commissioner, saw the Commissioner was indeed absent, and shut that door. He also shut the massive oak door that led to the outer rooms, then returned and sat in a deep upholstered chair opposite George Scott. Inspector Battle also sat down and watched Peter roll a brown-paper cigarette.

"Kind of a board of estimate ourselves," Peter repeated.

Scott gave him the wary look of a politician's watchdog, and said, "I didn't expect you to be out of the hospital so soon, Lieutenant." He sat on the edge of his chair and peered, first at Peter, then at Inspector Battle, then back at Peter again. "If you ask me, I think it's a mistake."

"What's a mistake?"

"Your leaving the hospital. You were fairly safe there. We might have arranged it so you could have been even safer."

"You mean put me away in a good well-furnished padded cell, with hot and cold packs?"

Scott gave a little repressed bookkeeperish snort, but said nothing.

"What did you think that would make me safe from?" asked Peter. "Or did you think it would make someone else safe?"

Inspector Battle coughed. In spite of his honesty and his fearlessness, he did not quite approve of flippancy in the office of high officials of the Department.

"I thought it would be safest for the Department," Scott said. "It would have saved us a great deal of embarrassment."

Peter's brown-paper cigarette burned to a black little end and went out. He reached over the desk and put it in the ash tray, which was expensive and ornate and had in its center a small statue of Hermes, messenger of the god, complete with winged hat and winged sandals.

"The good of the Department, eh?" said Peter.

"Well, frankly, Lieutenant," George Scott said with the beginning of an unpleasant gleam in his little eyes, ordinarily so benign, "we are glad to keep you out of trouble. But the first consideration is the Department. The individual is always secondary to the service."

"Harrumph!" said Peter.

"I beg your pardon?"

Inspector Battle turned his squarish hat around on his knees. Peter began rolling another cigarette, allowing the loose ends of tobacco to fall into the ash tray over Hermes' winged hat and down past Hermes' winged sandals.

"That's quite a nice ash tray," Peter said. "Unusual, too. Does it belong to the Department?"

Scott looked from Peter's eyes to the ashtray and then back to Peter's eyes again. The ashtray was uncommunicative and so were Peter's eyes.

"I had it made," said Scott.

"How interesting! Your own design?"

"Well, not exactly. But my own idea. I had a jeweler make it up the way I wanted it. Kind of a hobby."

"Well! That is fascinating. Have you had a lot of things made up like that? Little trinkets, with gods and goddesses on them?"

"Quite a few," said Scott, with something of his benign look stealing back over his face. "I get the ideas out of a book called *Bulfinch's Mythology*. Here's one my jeweler just made up for me." Scott took a fountain pen out of his inside coat pocket and showed it to Peter. It was of solid gold and the cap was surmounted by a small, exquisitely made head of a man.

"Who is it?" Peter asked. "Jupiter—or Bacchus?"

"Jupiter," Scott said, with a tinge of pride in his voice.

"Fascinating!" said Peter.

One of the telephones on Scott's desk rang and he answered it. "It's for you, Inspector."

Inspector Battle's conversation consisted of four words: "Hello," "Yes," and "All right." Both Peter and George watched him as he put the instrument back in its cradle. "Just the office," the Inspector said.

Peter crossed his legs and relaxed. "Solid gold, too," he remarked as he handed the pen back to Scott. "Must be a pretty expensive hobby—expensive for a Commissioner's secretary, that is. Solid gold and all that sort of thing."

"How I spend my salary is none of your business, Lieutenant Hanley," Scott said sharply.

"Now don't get me wrong," said Peter. "I'm not belittling your position one bit. It's a good job. A lot bigger job than you started with, in the nineteen-twenties, on Third Avenue."

"What do you mean?" Scott said.

"Well, let's be frank. You were just a small-time ward politician. You came up the hard way. Right?"

"I came up by being loyal to the party, since you seem to be interested."

"Exactly. But not too loyal. You were, in party matters, a good wheelhorse, but you made some interesting connections outside the party. Eventually you sort of worked the connections and the party together, didn't you? All the way up to and including the time you wangled yourself an appointment in the Commissioner's office."

Scott's eyes were bright and the red in his face was matched by the red around his neck. "What the hell are you trying to get at, Hanley?"

"Just a few facts." Peter began rolling another brown-paper cigarette, again spilling the remnants over Hermes' wings. "When you wanted me put away in a nuthouse for life, I began to get a little curious about you. Here and there, I began to add things up. Sometimes two and two made four, but oftener they made four and a half. But don't mind me."

The bookkeeperish look was quite gone and Scott's eyes were suddenly ablaze. "I'll have you put out of here," he cried, half rising.

"Sit down!" It was Inspector Battle who spoke, and his voice cut like a wind in November. Scott sat down.

"You won't have anybody put out," said Peter, lighting the ragged end of his cigarette. "You're all added up. You come out to eighteen and three-quarters. I must admit that while I was in that hospital I was a little foggy, and it took me quite a while to get the pieces put together, but finally I did."

There was a knock at the oaken door. Inspector Battle peered out, said something in a low voice, and, shutting the door again, resumed his place.

"Tell me one thing," said Peter. "When did you first make the acquaintance of Julius Hassenpepper?"

"That is an impertinent question! I'll—I'll take you before the Commissioner for this!"

"What an interesting reaction," Peter murmured. "Dr. Gatskill would find that very significant, I'm sure. Father image, or something. No, George, you won't take anybody before the Commissioner. Why don't you answer that question while you still have a chance to say something?"

"I never knew Julius Hassenpepper. Except in the last few years, when everybody knew him. Including Mr. Marriner, the present Commissioner, and Jim

Houlihan, the previous Commissioner."

"That is a damned lie. Why tell me lies, George?"

"I might have met him accidentally, in the old days."

"You might have met him accidentally in the old days. You knew him on Third Avenue, in the nineteen-twenties, when he was a two-bit bookie and you were a two-bit ward heeler. Isn't that so?"

Scott's little eyes, bright with hate and fear, went from Peter to Inspector Battle and back again. "You're very smart. You're the guy they called a hero cop. You got yourself mixed up in a murder and this is the way you're trying to get out. Trying to smear somebody else. Trying to smear me. Just a little guy. You always pick on the little guys."

"That, too," Peter said judicially, "is an interesting reaction. Dr. Gatskill would love it. A little guy. Just a little guy."

"You leave me alone!"

"One more question. Did anybody ever call you Porjie?"

"No!"

"It's odd they didn't. Sometimes little boys named George get that tagged on to them. Georgie-Porjie. Georgie-Porjie."

Scott started to rise again.

"Sit down!" It was Inspector Battle's voice again, and Scott sat down.

"Another question, please," said Peter. "I think this is really the last. Do you remember, when you came to visit me in the hospital, you were very curious to learn if I remembered having seen you any time the night Narcissa Maidstone was killed? I think, now that I've had time to think everything over, you were quite anxious and worried on that point. What Dr. Gatskill would call an anxiety state. Do you remember asking me that, George?"

"Yes."

"Well, here's your answer. I didn't see you. And the reason I didn't see you was the light was out."

Scott made a guttural little sound in his throat. "You're insane. Insane."

Peter Hanley leaned forward intently. "I'm going to give you a thumbnail sketch of yourself, Georgie-Porjie. You hooked up with Julius Hassenpepper in the twenties, in Prohibition days. He supplied the cash and the know-how. You supplied the connections. With the officials, with the cops, with everybody, with the party. This little alliance prospered. It prospered until Julius was a big shot on his side and you were a big shot on your side. You were only a secretary, still getting paid off with political jobs like this one, but when it came to influence you were a big shot. You were both big shots. And both of you kept getting on the other side of the fence. Julius began thinking he was a politician and you thought you were a big shot gambler.

"And then somewhere along the line you got the idea into your head that you ought to have a bigger share. Once you got that idea the next idea was to eliminate Julius from the picture. In the kind of business you were in when you say eliminate you mean eliminate. A slug of lead is the best little old eliminator you can think of. And that is where Shorty Cerwin came into the picture."

Peter leaned back and folded a cigarette paper into the shape of a paper airplane. He sailed it across the room and began making another. Scott, flushed, his eyes bright, sat still, his fingers clutched on the arms of his chair. Inspector Battle turned his squarish pipe over and over in his long fingers.

"That is where Shorty Cerwin came into the picture,"

Peter repeated softly, "and that was where Narcissa Maidstone came in, too. Shorty was a hanger-on of the Hassenpepper mob, and Narcissa was a sort of hanger-on, too. Indeed, she was not at all the girl I fondly thought she was. She was as cold-blooded as they come, and where she came into the picture was that you sent her along with Shorty Cerwin to see that he did the job. You promised them big shares in the empire that you were going to inherit. Oddly enough, they never got any of the shares. Shorty Cerwin burned at Sing Sing. And Narcissa Maidstone? Nobody knows better than you what happened to her."

"You're insane!"

"No. Not insane. Just a little whacky. Now listen to the rest of the thumbnail sketch. After Shorty Cerwin went to the chair you were still afraid. You saw that we were still prowling around, that we weren't satisfied we had come to the real end of the trail. So what did you do? You put Narcissa Maidstone on to me. She was your spy. Your spy, to see what I knew, to warn you if it ever looked as though we were going to reopen the case. Isn't that right?"

"No!" Scott's knuckles were white as he clutched the chair.

"Well, I guess lying won't hurt you. It's the least of your sins. But you *are* lying. And then, as has happened many a time before, you got worried about your spy. You began to be afraid of the double-cross. Because, if Narcissa Maidstone should give you the double-cross, that would really be the end. You watched her like a hawk, and finally you got it into your head that she was falling in love with me. That was the danger you feared. Because you knew that a woman in love is dangerous, not to be trusted. Whether she was falling in love with me is beside the point.

Personally, I don't think she was. I don't think she had it in her. Not love. But you were afraid she was.

"So, having eliminated Julius Hassenpepper, you now thought it high time you eliminated Narcissa. Whether you planned doing it at the particular moment, I don't know. It doesn't matter. You came to talk to her, discovered me there. You reacted with fear and hatred. Those emotions are practically the same thing, anyhow. Dr. Gatskill would tell you that. And, reacting with fear and hatred, you tackled us both. Unfortunately for you, I lived through it."

George Scott was up out of his chair now. The desk drawer was open. Peter found himself looking straight into the muzzle of a small-caliber pistol. Scott's eyes now held no trace of benignity; on the contrary, they were small and mean and cruel.

"There are two of you," Scott said in a thin voice, "but now I have what they call the equalizer. I think it more than equalizes. Anyway, there better not be any funny business in here. That door is two inches thick and the walls even more." His voice dropped to a whisper. "You could die on that floor with a bullet in your gut and nobody would know the difference. Do you understand that?"

Peter wondered if Scott was bluffing, and decided that he wasn't. The walls were indeed thick, the room well insulated and deadened to sounds, and outside the Municipal Building there was the full morning roar of downtown Manhattan. "In a minute we are going to walk out of this room," Scott continued, "and you two will be ahead of me. Nobody will be the wiser—unless you try something funny. And then it won't matter. Because you will be dead men and I'll be on my way."

Peter's eyes met Inspector Battle's briefly. Then

George Scott put the pistol in his pocket, keeping his fingers rightly upon it.

Suddenly Inspector Battle shot upward from his chair, made a swift lunge across the desk. There was a sharp little report. Inspector Battle grunted, seemed to grapple with a phantom, and pitched without a sound across the edge of the desk to the floor.

"See what I mean?" said Scott.

Peter watched him, watched the little spiral of smoke that rose lazily in the air from the newly burned hole in the pepper-and-salt coat. "You made a hell of a mistake there, George," Peter said. "If you and I go out of here, Inspector Battle will tell on you. Alive or dead, he'll tell on you."

A little speck of foam came to Scott's lips. He wiped it away with a nervous gesture of his left hand.

"Nobody will find out—soon enough. I'll be too far away."

"You said I was crazy," Peter remarked. "It's you who are crazy. Clear out of your mind. Because you can't possibly get away with this."

Then Peter moved swiftly, much more swiftly than Inspector Battle had moved. He lunged across the desk, and both his hands closed like vises on Scott's right wrist. He had gauged it cautiously. It was a thing he had been trained to do. Scott fought with the fury of a cornered animal.

They closed and Scott managed to get his free arm around Peter's neck. Then they went struggling across the room, a chair tipped over, and they were against the window. For a moment Scott had Peter backed against the sill, and a good push would have sent him hurtling thirteen stories down to Chambers Street. But Peter's training and superior strength prevented that, and with a sudden twist he broke Scott's grip on the pistol and sent it spinning to the floor. He slid under Scott's arm and dived for the weapon, and came up, in a sitting position, with the pistol sighted across his knees and the sights between Scott's eyes.

"That was a nice game, Georgie. Very exciting. But you ought not to play games like that with a copper. I've been playing them a lot longer than you have. Taking a pistol from a man is something I learned way back in kindergarten."

Scott was shaking with fear and unaccustomed exertion.

"And now—" said Peter.

On the floor, Inspector Battle began to stir. He crept to his knees and after a moment he staggered to his feet.

"Get down, Inspector, and take it easy. You're hurt."

"Not so badly hurt I can't put the handcuffs on this fellow." And he did so.

"Now," said Peter, "I wonder if the committee is outside."

Inspector Battle was already opening the door. There was quite a little crowd there: two detectives from Homicide, Peckham and Anderson, in front and a couple of uniformed officers behind. Between them was a gaunt girl, terror in her eyes. She was Minnie Osler, Narcissa Maidstone's maid.

"Thanks for rounding her up," said Peter. "How about the other one? Dibble?"

Peckham shrugged his shoulders. "No luck yet. She's just as slippery as she always was. I've got a hunch we won't find her at all."

"Why?" Peter asked sharply.

Peckham made a motion with his forefinger, aiming it like a pistol at his head.

"No!" Peter said. "Not her. We'll find her, all right."

Minnie Osler was staring, not at Peter Hanley or Inspector Battle, but at the man who stood between them. George Scott, whose eyes were alive with fear, hatred, and reptilian venom.

"Don't let him near me!" she cried in an awful little voice. "Don't let him do to me what he did to her!"

"He won't hurt you, Minnie," said Peter. "We're just drawing his fangs."

For a moment the only sound was Scott's heavy breathing. Then Peter said with a commanding tone, "Now off with you. Off with you all."

The little party left the outer ring of the inner sanctum, and they all disappeared among the outer doors, while the brass—the small brass and the medium brass—stared at them and stared at the vacant space they had occupied. Inspector Battle left for the hospital to have his flesh wound treated, while Peter decided to wait until the Commissioner returned, as he felt he owed him an explanation for having removed his Executive Secretary and watchdog.

While he waited, rays of the late afternoon sun, slanting across the corner windows from City Hall Park, glanced off something in the open drawer of George Scott's desk. It was a round golden object; a lady's compact etched with the likeness of Diana. Refraction made the intaglio profile seem to light up a bit. Diana, Goddess of the Hunt, was almost smiling.

27

He was in the corner room, overlooking the rose garden of the University, packing his clothes. It was a fair September day and there were tennis players in the court opposite; he could hear their cries of "Love-fifteen!" "Love-thirty!" and "Love-forty!" When he had got the last shirt stuffed into his suitcase and was searching the maple chest of drawers for overlooked items, Miss Lupino came in. She gave him a bright professional smile.

"I hear you're leaving us for good."

"Yes, unless we change our minds."

"Dr. Gatskill is on the floor," said Miss Lupino. "I expect she wants to talk to you before you go."

"I expect she does," said Peter.

But Dr. Gatskill did not come in at once. Instead, Milt DeBaer and Brian arrived after a game of badminton.

"I hear they're springing you," said Brian.

"True enough," said Peter.

"Congratulations!" cried Brian. "Or—come to think of it, I don't know. This ain't a bad place, when you get right down to it. A hell of a lot better than the Army. You know what?"

"What?"

"They're talking about kicking me out. They think I'm forming a neurotic attachment for the place. How do you like that?"

Milton DeBaer, in an excess of spirits, pumped Peter's hand.

"Nice to've known you," he said. "Nice to've known you."

Then Brian said, "Your girlfriend's leaving, too."

"Girlfriend? Who?"

"Helen."

"Oh. I guess I ought to say good-by."

"Too late. She's gone down in the elevator. You might see her out in front, though."

Peter looked out the window and saw Helen in the

forecourt, about to get into a taxi. She looked smaller and more little-girlish than ever. He whistled and she looked up.

"Good-by!" he called. "Good-by—and good luck!"

Helen waved and said something, but Peter could not hear what it was. Then she got into the taxi and was gone.

Brian and Milt DeBaer shook his hand again and went out. After a while Dr. Gatskill came in. She gazed at him with a faraway twinkle in her eyes.

"How do you feel about leaving?" she asked.

"I feel fine."

"Do you really feel fine? Or are you just telling me that?"

"You sound like Dr. Holmka," said Peter. "Yes. I really feel fine. Everything is all right. Don't you think so?"

"I think you have done very well." The bell-like tones were soft and faraway. "You are the kind of patient we like to have, Lieutenant Hanley."

"Thanks."

"I wish you all the luck and success in the world."

"Thanks again. The same to you."

Dr. Gatskill sat on the edge of the bed and watched him finish his packing. "Do you mind if I ask a couple of questions?"

Peter grinned. "No. I'm hardened to it."

"Tell me—what was it that first put you onto the trail of that terrible little man, Scott?"

Peter drew a strap tight and buckled it. "There were a good many things. They all came along, and I have to think what it was that came first. Some of them were way out of the background, things I'd known a long time ago and forgotten."

"Things like what?"

"Well, in the first place I must remind you again

that police work is chiefly concerned with small and insignificant details. A little like psychiatry, maybe. A detective stores a lot of these details in his mind, in a sort of rough filing system. Sometimes they're stored pretty far back, and he doesn't get at them all at once, but usually they come out of their little compartments sooner or later."

"What kind of things did you have filed away about this man?"

"Well, in the first place, I had always known that in his early days Julius Hassenpepper was tied up with a character called 'Porjie.' He was a ward politician of a very low order and he never got into the picture very much, but he was in it just the same."

"That didn't link anything up to Scott," she said.

"No. Not directly. But I linked them up when I got out of here and could do a little checking from Headquarters. I found that Porjie and George Scott were the same."

"What brought it up in the first place?"

"I remembered, in the depths of that amytal nonsense, that Narcissa, just before she was killed, had cried 'Porjie!' Naturally, when I remembered that, I got to wondering who Porjie was. Then, later on, I recalled the Porjie in Hassenpepper's background. Really, all it took then was to check the files and do a little general fiddling around. If I could find out what had happened to Porjie, I could have a very good idea who killed Narcissa.

"Actually, I already had an inkling of where my man was. That also came out of the back drawers of my mental filing cabinet. I haven't been in the Commissioner's office too many times, but I had been there often enough. And I remembered that fantastic ash tray, with the figure of Hermes in the center of it.

It finally clicked. The intaglio compact with Diana on it, and the ash tray with Hermes in the middle. They all added up."

"I should think so," said Dr. Gatskill. "What an odd character this Scott was!"

"And, in his way, quite clever," said Peter. "He had his hands on half the money in New York City, but he never flashed any of it. Except indirectly. He had this weakness for bric-a-brac, and it was this, I guess, more than anything, that spilled him."

"You remembered the name Porjie, and you remembered the bric-a-brac. What else?"

"I remembered how anxious Scott had been to know if I had seen him the night Narcissa was killed. It was a bold thing for him to do, to ask me, but he had to do it. He had to know. He was counting on my dazed condition, and he was counting on my not having seen him. At first glance, his visit to me in the hospital was innocent enough. The Commissioner might very well have sent him to find out what was what. But on second glance, it was not so innocent at all."

"Speaking of the Commissioner," said Dr. Gatskill, "what about this affair Narcissa said she had with him? Where did that connect up?"

"It didn't. It all happened a long time ago, before Marriner was Police Commissioner. It didn't connect up to Hassenpepper or Scott. Just one of those things. I checked it all out."

"I think you are very clever," Dr. Gatskill said gravely.

"No, not clever at all. It was just a question of luck. Bullheaded luck—and psychotherapy, I guess. It was a question of remembering things I had forgotten."

"And you remembered the maid, too. Minnie What's-her-name."

"Yes. I remembered her. That was important, really

important. Because nobody—except George Scott and I—really knew that she existed. I was certain she was an important link, once I remembered that she must have seen the murderer. And having seen him, I knew she would have taken a powder. Because if she had even half an ounce of brains she'd have known she was next."

"Where did you locate her?"

"Oh, she was hiding with a sister in Brooklyn. We got her just in time, too, because half an hour after we got her out of there we picked up a couple of Scott's hoods in a car parked across from her apartment."

"Was she in on it?"

"Oh, yes. Definitely. She had been one of Scott's hangers-on for a long time. She was planted in the apartment to keep an eye on Narcissa."

"Setting a spy to spy on a spy."

"Exactly."

"And what about the nurse? Our Miss Dibble? Did you ever find her, and where did she fit in?"

"She was picked up a couple of hours ago at Idlewild, ready to take off for Paris. And George was with her. You remember George?"

"What George?"

"The orderly. The ersatz orderly who shoved me out the window."

"Oh, him! Were these two operating for Scott?"

"Not primarily, although Scott knew what was going on and gave some help to Dibble. Dibble's motive was revenge. She hated me with a cold and terrible hate, and she wanted to kill me."

"Why?"

"She was Shorty Cerwin's girlfriend. You remember: I sent Shorty Cerwin to the chair—as the trigger man in the Hassenpepper murder. At the time of the trial we tried to locate his girlfriend, whom we knew to have been a trained nurse. As it turned out, she was trained in your specialty, as a psychiatric nurse. We never found her, never even knew her exact identity, but it didn't matter too much then; we didn't really need her for the trial."

"Then, when she heard you were here, she saw her opportunity, re-registered as a nurse, and got us to give her a job."

"That's right. Then she managed to get a patient whom she knew to be homicidal, especially on the subject of cops, onto the floor and hoped for the worst. When that failed, she got George in to do the job. He was Cerwin's brother, from the looks of him, but the way I was feeling then, all mixed up, groggy, I didn't notice it. Didn't occur to me. But when George muffed it she decided to do it herself, and an overdose of amytal seemed like just the right thing."

"It was, from her standpoint," Dr. Gatskill said. "Your system was already full of it, and you couldn't stand much more. Lucky we caught you in time, and lucky you have a very rugged constitution."

"Yes," Peter said. "Lucky. Very lucky."

He picked up his suitcase and his small traveling bag and set them beside the door.

"There's just one minor thing I'd like to know," said Dr. Gatskill. "You remember this girl, this Narcissa, first met you on some pretext or another. She had some kind of a problem, and you could never remember what it was. Did you ever remember that?"

Peter was silent for a moment, and embarrassed.

"Yes, I remembered. It was such a silly thing that I'd just as soon forget it again."

"What was it?"

He grinned sheepishly. "Well, all it was, was this.

She wanted me to fix a traffic ticket."

"A what? A traffic ticket! Oh, that's really wonderful!" And Dr. Gatskill's laughter ran all around the room.

Peter smiled and moved toward the door. Dr. Gatskill got up and followed him; the violet eyes came nearer. And now there was a warm light in them, as suddenly she took Peter's hand and pressed it for a moment, pressed it tightly and warmly.

"Please take care of yourself," she said, and in a moment she was gone, the violet eyes were gone and the bell-like voice was gone. There was a swish of starched white gown and the twinkle of blue shoes, and Dr. Gatskill was gone. Peter stood staring at his hand; he could still feel the warmth of the handclasp.

He picked up his things and went into the corridor, but she was gone from sight. But as he passed along toward the doors to the elevators, he met Dr. Holmka. Peter started to speak, but he saw that Dr. Holmka did not recognize him, was lost in abstraction as he walked, his gown swinging with his stride, his notepad in one hand and his gold pen in the other. Dr. Holmka's eyes, cool and blue as the fjords, looked at Peter and beyond him, far beyond him, and Dr. Holmka passed on.

At the door which led to the elevators, Peter stood and waited for someone to come and open it. But the floor was quiet, and he could hear the sounds from the outside. A tug hooted on the river, and along the East River Drive a chorus of elfin taxi horns hooted in reply. A golden bar of reflected sunshine lay across the door, and then Peter touched the knob. Peter touched the door and it opened. The door opened.

THE END

Paul Eugene Conant was born in San Bernardino, California, in 1906. He worked as a copy reader in Fort Lewis, Washington, in 1942. He wrote one novel under his own name and two under the name Gene Paul (both published by Lion Books). Conant died in New York in 1968.

BLACK GAT BOOKS offers the best in reprint crime fiction from the 1950s-1970s. New titles appear every month, and each book is sized to 4.25" x 7", just like they used to be. Collect them all.

- Harry Whittington · A Haven for the Damned #1 ·
- Charlie Stella · Eddie's World #2
- Leigh Brackett · Stranger at Home #3
- John Flagg · The Persian Cat #4
- Malcolm Braly · Felony Tank #6
- Vin Packer · The Girl on the Best Seller List #7
- Orrie Hitt · She Got What She Wanted #8
- Helen Nielsen · The Woman on the Roof #9
- Lou Cameron · Angel's Flight #10
- Gary Lovisi · The Affair of Lady Westcott's Lost Ruby / The Case of the Unseen Assassin #11
- Arnold Hano · The Last Notch #12
- Clifton Adams · Never Say No to a Killer #13
- Ed Lacy · The Men From the Boys #14
- Henry Kane · Frenzy of Evil #15
- William Ard · You'll Get Yours #16
- Bert & Dolores Hitchens · End of the Line #17
- Noël Calef · Frantic #18
- Ovid Demaris · The Hoods Take Over #19
- Fredric Brown · Madball #20
- Louis Malley Stool Pigeon #21
- Frank Kane · The Living End #22
- Ferguson Findley · My Old Man's Badge #23
- Paul Connolly · Tears are for Angels #24
- E. P. Fenwick · Two Names for Death #25
- Lorenz Heller · Dead Wrong #26
- Robert Martin · Little Sister #27
- Calvin Clements · Satan Takes the Helm #28
- Jack Karney · Cut Me In #29
- George Benet · The Hoodlums #30
- Jonathan Craig · So Young, So Wicked #31
- Edna Sherry · Tears for Jessie Hewitt #32
- William O'Farrell · Repeat Performance #33
- Marvin Albert · The Girl With No Place to Hide #34
- Edward S. Aarons · Gang Rumble #35
- William Fuller · Back Country #36
- Robert Silverberg · The Killer #37
- William R. Cox · Make My Coffin Strong #38
- A. S. Fleischman · Blood Alley #39
- Harold R. Daniels · The Girl in 304 #40
- William H. Duhart - The Deadly Pay-Off #41
- Robert Ames - Awake and Die #42
- Charles Runyon - Object of Lust #43

Stark House Press
1315 H Street, Eureka, CA 95501 (707) 498-3135
griffinskye3@sbcglobal.net www.starkhousepress.com
Available from your local bookstore or direct from the publisher

www.ingramcontent.com/pod-product-compliance
Lightning Source LLC
LaVergne TN
LVHW021818060526
838201LV00058B/3426